BACK TO THE TITANIC!

BACK TO THE TITANIC!

Beatrice Gormley

AN
APPLE
PAPERBACK

SCHOLASTIC INC.
New York Toronto London Auckland Sydney

ISBN 0-590-46226-1

12 11 10 9 8 7 6 5   4 5 6 7 8 9/9

Printed in the U.S.A.   40

First Scholastic printing, April 1994

Contents

BACK TO THE TITANIC!

The R.M.S. *Titanic*

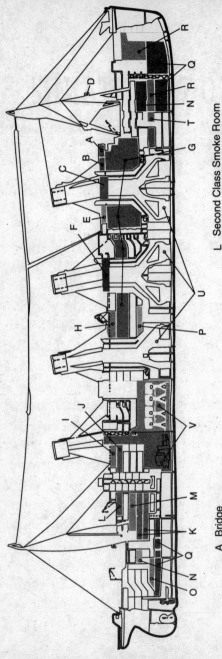

A Bridge
B Wheelhouse
C Officers' Quarters
D Crow's Nest
E Wireless Room
F Gymnasium
G First Class State Rooms
H First Class Lounge
I First Class Smoke Room
J First Class Restaurant
K Second Class State Rooms

L Second Class Smoke Room
M Second Class Dining Saloon
N Third Class Berths
O Third Class Common Room
P Third Class Dining Room
Q Cargo
R Crews' Quarters
S Motor Cars
T Post Mail Room
U Boilers
V Engines

1.
A Survivor of the
Titanic

Matt Cowen wasn't looking forward to visiting his great-grandfather, but he guessed it was the right thing to do. Matt and his friend Jonathan Schultz, both twelve, were walking up the cement path to Grandpa Frank's front porch. Ahead of them Emily, Matt's ten-year-old sister, charged up the steps, her red hair bouncing. She was carrying a container of soup.

"Maybe I should go get my skateboard and meet you at the park." Jonathan hung back, folding his long, skinny arms as if to protect himself.

"Get on up here." Matt swung his arm. "Don't be a jerk." But Matt felt sad and nervous, himself. What had his mother meant, warning him that his great-grandfather might be "lost in his thoughts about the *Titanic*"?

Matt wasn't used to worrying about Grandpa Frank. He wasn't even used to walking across the creaking boards of the front porch. When he and Jonathan came by to see Grandpa Frank, they never rang the front doorbell. They went straight down the driveway to the workshop in the garage.

On a nice April afternoon like this, with robins hopping across the lawn, the door of the garage should be up. The old man should be in there, peering from under his baseball cap at the project on his workbench.

"He might not want to see me," grumbled Jonathan in Matt's ear. "He's not *my* great-grandfather. Besides, I don't know what to say."

"You say, 'Hey, Mr. Kenny, I'm sorry you broke your leg.' Duh! Of course he wants to see you, man." Jonathan might be a sixth-grade science star, thought Matt, but he didn't know the first thing about people's feelings.

Emily had already rung the doorbell. Mrs. Wilson, the housekeeper, opened the door. "Aren't you kids sweet, coming to visit your poor great-grandpa." She gave a sigh. "If only he'd waited for you to get the photographs of the ship, instead of climbing up on that ladder himself! He actually asked *me* to climb up, but I said, 'Mr. Kenny,' I said — "

"Here's some soup from Mom, for Grandpa." Emily pushed the container at Mrs. Wilson.

"Excuse us," said Matt. Talking to Mrs. Wilson was another thing that he and Jonathan wouldn't do ordinarily.

The housekeeper took the soup and stepped out of their way, but she continued to cluck. "You mustn't be upset if he doesn't know you. Well, what can you expect. He's nearly ninety, after all."

Jonathan looked alarmed and pulled back again, but Matt grabbed his friend's skinny arm. "Never mind Mrs. Wilson," he whispered. "She always talks doom and gloom."

Emily cast a glance at Mrs. Wilson as if to say that the housekeeper wasn't so young, herself. She strode down the hall with a flip of her red curls. The door of the back bedroom was half open, showing the foot of the bed and an aluminum walker. Emily knocked.

"It's not too late!" came their great-grandfather's voice.

Emily turned to raise her eyebrows at her brother. "It's not too late" did seem like an odd way to say "Come in," but Matt shrugged. He pushed Jonathan into the room in front of him.

Grandpa Frank's bedroom was dark and stuffy. The old man, propped up by pillows, lay on top of the bed. The cast on his right leg stuck straight out under his plaid bathrobe. Without his usual baseball cap, the top of Grandpa Frank's head looked very bald and spotted. The hearing aid in his leathery right ear was more noticeable, too.

"Hi, Grandpa," said Matt. He wondered if that hearing aid was turned on. The old man was wearing his glasses and staring straight ahead at the TV on the dresser, although the screen was blank.

Emily went around to the other side of the bed and hugged the old man, kissing his folded cheek. "Mom sent you some homemade soup."

"Hey, Mr. Kenny," said Jonathan, his narrow face solemn. "I'm sorry you broke your leg."

"It's not too late," repeated Grandpa Frank, still staring at the gray TV screen as if he were watching a movie. "Warn the captain — ice! Binoculars to the lookout! Ram the iceberg head on!"

"This isn't funny, Grandpa," said Emily.

But Matt didn't think their great-grandfather was pretending. "Lost in his thoughts," Mom had said — lost in time, was more like it. It sounded like Grandpa Frank thought he was actually back on the *Titanic*, the famous "unsinkable" ocean liner on its way from England to New York in 1912. Many immigrants, including the young Frank Kenny, had set out on that voyage.

Matt tried to imagine his grandfather on the *Titanic*, but he could only picture his own round face at the age of six, with his curious gray-blue eyes and springy, sandy brown hair. They didn't have any photos of Grandpa Frank as a boy.

Grandpa Frank would never talk to the kids about the *Titanic*, either. Matt, who loved history, had asked him about it several times. When Matt was in third grade, he'd first heard about the sinking of the *Titanic* — and learned that his own great-grandfather had almost gone down with that ship.

Since then, Matt had been fascinated by the ship. He had tried every so often to get Grandpa Frank to talk about the *Titanic*. One year he'd ask, "What was it like, Grandpa, when the ship was sinking?" The next year, "Why do you think the ship hit that iceberg?"

Each time Matt asked, Grandpa Frank's kindly face would harden, and sometimes he walked out of the room. He had never answered.

Now Matt fidgeted, wanting to do something, he didn't know what. Jonathan's dark eyes darted around as if he knew exactly what he wanted to be doing — skateboarding in the park.

Grandpa Frank spoke again, in a voice like a sleepy boy's. "It's nighttime, Aunt Rose. Why must we get up?"

Then an imitation of a woman's voice, with an Irish lilt, came from the old man's mouth: "Hush, lad! On with your clothes, quick as quick."

Matt's skin crawled. He glanced across the bed at Emily. Her face was even paler than usual as she stared at Grandpa Frank. "What are you talking about?" she asked.

The old man didn't seem to hear Emily. He panted, as if he'd been running. He spoke in still another voice, a man's: "The mail room's swamped. She's sinking fast. Up to the boats!"

The boats. Matt knew that meant the lifeboats. And he knew that there hadn't been enough lifeboats on the Royal Mail Ship *Titanic*. After it hit the iceberg on the night of April 14, 1912, the *Titanic* had sunk to the bottom of the Atlantic Ocean a few hours later. Hundreds of people had gone down with the ship. Young Frank Kenny had been one of the lucky ones to get away in a lifeboat.

Now the old man squeezed his eyes shut and opened them again. He blinked through his glasses from Emily to Jonathan to Matt. "I must have dozed off," he muttered in his own raspy voice. "You been here long? Have a seat, have a seat."

"You were talking like you were having nightmares," Emily told him.

"Hey, Mr. Kenny," said Jonathan, looking relieved. "I'm sorry you broke your leg." He perched his lanky form on the footboard of the bed.

The old man raised his eyebrows at the cast

6

on his own leg. "Not as sorry as I am, believe me. I had plans."

"What were you going to do?" asked Matt, sliding into a chair beside the night table.

Grandpa Frank shook his head, as if that thought were a mosquito biting him. "It's no use talking about it now." He narrowed his eyes around the room at each of the kids. "Well! It's kind of you to visit an old geezer with a broken leg. But shouldn't you be in school?"

"No, it's spring vacation." Emily plopped herself on the bed, near the pillows.

Matt thought how strange it seemed to see his great-grandfather's knobby, veiny hands lying on the bedspread, instead of gripping a screwdriver or a wrench. "Mrs. Wilson said you climbed up on a ladder in the garage to get pictures?"

Then Matt wished he hadn't said that, because the old man's face twisted. Matt thought he must be remembering breaking his leg. "I'm sorry," said Matt. "Never mind."

But Grandpa Frank fixed him with a sudden fierce gaze. "I was almost *there,* so close. . . ." He stretched out one trembling hand. "I could have stopped it, made everything right. . . . And then I had to fall off the dad-blasted ladder! My chance is gone. I might as well give up."

"Don't give up!" Emily put a hand on his shoulder, as if to shake him.

7

The old man patted her hand, but he didn't answer. He sighed deeply. Then he seemed to notice Jonathan, still perched on the footboard of the bed. In a calmer tone of voice Grandpa Frank asked, "Did you ever read a book, fellow by the name of Wells, *The Time Machine*?"

"Sure." Jonathan smiled. He loved to talk about science fiction. "The evolution part was kind of boring, but the time machine was cool — those crystal bars with the weird twist to them."

"Mm-hm," said Grandpa Frank. "The crystal, that's what set me to thinking. Of course the whole notion of traveling *on* the machine was wrong."

"Time travel is impossible anyway, though," said Jonathan. He leaned forward, and a lock of his straight, dark hair fell over his forehead. "Say you found a gap in the space-time fabric, like maybe a black hole. The closer you get to the hole, the more packed-together matter becomes. So way before you even reach the point where you'd come out in some other space and time, you're totally squished." He spoke in a regretful tone, pushing his hair off his forehead. "Bones, muscles, everything — Jell-O pudding."

"Gross," said Matt. He and Emily made sick faces at each other.

Grandpa Frank only smiled to himself. "You know just about everything, do you, son?" he asked Jonathan. "And you're only in the sixth

8

grade. Well, *I* never went to college, but I know a thing or two." His smile faded, and he grimaced. "Not that it's going to do me or anyone else a lick of good, now. It's too late."

"Does your leg hurt, Grandpa?" asked Emily. "I'm sorry — I was bouncing around. Want me to get off the bed?"

Grandpa Frank shook his head, and he patted her hand again. "You stay right where you are, honey. It only hurts up here." He tapped the side of his head. "Some terrible things that happened, they didn't *have* to happen. I could still save them all, if only . . ."

"Save who?" asked Emily. "If only, what?"

But the old man's eyes clouded over. He shut them and let his head fall back on the pillows. When he opened his eyes again, he stared past Jonathan to the TV screen.

"She's sliding under at the bow. Dear God!" The last words were forced out in a groan. "So many people left on board — crowding like sheep up toward the stern . . ."

Emily gave Matt a worried look. He was worried, too. Should he go call his mother at her office?

But at that moment, Mrs. Wilson bustled in, carrying a glass of water and a pill. "Time for your sedative, Mr. Kenny." The housekeeper took in their dismayed expressions. "Has he been going on about the ship? Tsk, tsk." She

9

shook her head. "I'm afraid his mind may never be right again."

"Come on," said Matt to Emily and Jonathan. He was glad to leave the dark, stuffy bedroom, glad to stop watching his great-grandfather suffer. At the same time, he wanted so badly to do something for Grandpa Frank.

In the hall Emily said, "Poor Grandpa!" She sniffled, wiping her eyes with the cuff of her sweatshirt. "It's like he's having nightmares, and he can't wake up."

"Why's he so upset about the *Titanic*?" There was a concerned look in Jonathan's brown eyes. "It happened so many years ago — you'd think he'd be over it by now."

Matt shook his head. "My mother thinks he never *started* to get over it. He just blanked the whole thing out of his mind. When she was a kid, she didn't even know he was a survivor of the *Titanic*."

"Weird," commented Jonathan.

"Then, a while ago," Matt went on, "they discovered the *Titanic* at the bottom of the ocean, and someone came and tried to interview Grandpa for a TV show. And that started him brooding about the shipwreck."

"Grandpa on TV?" asked Emily. "I don't remember that."

"That's because he *wasn't* on TV. He wouldn't talk to them." Matt paused with his hand on the front doorknob. "Hold on. We're supposed to check in the workshop for our blender. Mom thought he might have finished fixing it."

"Who cares about the stupid blender?" asked Emily. "I just want Grandpa to act normal again."

Matt felt the same way. Besides, he didn't really want to go into Grandpa Frank's workshop without the old man. But Jonathan's eyes lit up, and he turned away from the door. "We *definitely* have to check the workshop. Come on."

Puzzled by the excited note in his friend's voice, Matt followed him back through the house. "Why?"

"What do you care about our blender?" asked Emily.

Jonathan paused in the kitchen, facing Matt and Emily. "Did you see how Mr. Kenny smiled like he had a secret, when we were talking about time travel? He thinks he's really on to something."

Turning the back door handle, Matt snorted. "On to something? On to the *Titanic*, you mean."

Jonathan shook his head. In long-legged strides he led the way across the lawn to the old one-car garage. "On to some kind of secret project, I bet you anything." He opened the side door of the garage. April sunshine poured into the shadowy workshop, and the smells of machine oil and musty wood wafted out.

Grandpa Frank didn't have a car anymore, so he had plenty of room in the garage for various machines and appliances, more or less taken apart: an old push lawn mower, a vacuum cleaner, a radio. Cartons of smaller gadgets, motors, and odd parts were stacked around the floor.

"I don't see our blender." Emily poked in a carton.

Matt pulled the chain on the fluorescent light above the workbench that ran the length of one wall. The light flickered, then lit up a scattering of tools and parts. A pad of lined paper on a clipboard was covered with Grandpa Frank's spidery scrawl and spotted with oily fingerprints.

On the other side of the garage, in a clearing among the cartons and machines, a stepladder stood under the rafters. Raising his eyes, Matt noticed a shoebox up there. Grandpa must have been trying to get it down when he fell. Matt winced, imagining the old man's shinbone cracking as he struck the cement floor.

"Ahem." Jonathan stood at the far end of the workbench. He rested one hand on a gray barbecue grill cover, which hid most of a metal cart.

"What?" asked Matt. "Oh, that thing he never lets us touch."

"Yeah. I'm going to take the cover off, okay?"

"No!" exclaimed Emily. She darted around

cartons to put her hands protectively on the cover. "If Grandpa said not to touch it, don't touch it."

Matt hurried toward the cart. "Relax, Em. Jonathan's not going to hurt anything. You know Grandpa lets Jonathan help him work on all kinds of stuff."

"Don't you want to see what it is?" Jonathan coaxed Emily. "I bet this is what he meant, when he said he was almost there."

"Well — " Emily hesitated. "If we just *look* . . ."

Jonathan pulled the cover off. The three of them stared.

"Jeez." Jonathan snorted. "Did he do this for the middle-school science fair, or what? This is the weirdest mixed-up mess."

Matt blinked at the contraption before them, clumps of machines and instruments bolted and clamped and wired to the shelves of the metal cart. "I told you. He's losing it."

"I don't know," said Emily. "The things Grandpa fixes always look sort of patched together. But they work."

Jonathan bent over the cart, peering at the largest object on the top shelf. "This looks like it used to be an opaque projector. But he's made some adjustments. And he's fitted something over the lens. Some kind of pink crystal."

"That's the same color as the stone in a necklace of Mom's." Emily peered under Jonathan's arm. "Rose quartz."

Jonathan picked up a small flat object from beside the projector. "What's this remote control thing supposed to do?" he asked himself. "I wish he'd left directions."

"I saw some notes on the workbench." Matt hopped back over the cartons to the bench and picked up the clipboard. "Whoa, his writing! It's like Chinese." He returned more slowly, frowning at the notes.

Jonathan looked over Matt's shoulder at the spidery scrawls, while Emily squinted over Matt's other arm. Jonathan shook his head. "Looks like *'Fine and'* — what?"

Matt couldn't make it out, either. But Emily began reading in her clear, high voice. " *'Time and Space Connector (TASC). One.'* "

"How can you read it off, just like that?" Matt interrupted. "You must be making it up."

"No, I'm not." Emily looked up, her light blue eyes flashing. "I can read it. You just have to squint at it out of the corner of your eye."

"Listen!" exclaimed Jonathan. He pulled back from Matt and Emily and gripped the top shelf of the cart. "Don't you get it? This is what Mr. Kenny was hinting about. About going back and saving everybody. This invention" — he tapped the metal shelf — "is a way to travel through time."

2.
The "If Onlys"

"Oh, right," said Emily scornfully. "I just heard you tell Grandpa how *nobody* could travel through time."

Jonathan shrugged. "I'm not saying this Time and Space Connector — TASC, Mr. Kenny calls it for short — would work. Just that that's what he thinks he's built." But there was a gleam in Jonathan's dark eyes. "See these clocks?" He pointed to two digital clocks on the middle shelf. "What date do you think they're set for?"

Matt pressed a button to read the date on one of the clocks. "Today's date, April fourteenth. What's the big deal?"

Emily pressed the button for the calendar function on the other clock. "April fourteenth . . . nineteen-twelve," she read slowly.

Nineteen-twelve. Matt felt goose bumps. "That's the date the *Titanic* hit the iceberg."

"See?" asked Jonathan. "Maybe that was why he was in such a hurry to get whatever" — he

15

waved a hand at the shoebox in the rafters — "that he fell off the ladder. He thought he had to finish this by today."

Emily's mouth hung open. "Because he had to *use* it today?"

"To travel back to the *Titanic*?" added Matt. "He *is* losing it!" He stared at the contraption his great-grandfather had built. A way to travel into the past.

That didn't make any sense. The word itself, "past," meant that it was over and done with, didn't it? On the other hand, sitting with Grandpa Frank a little while ago, Matt had almost believed he was listening to a drama taking place right now. Inside the old man's head, at least, the *Titanic* was sinking *now*. The seawater was lapping at the stairs, the deck was tilting.

As Matt wrestled with these thoughts, Jonathan pulled the clipboard with Grandpa Frank's notes out of his hands and gave it to Emily. Emily began to read the notes aloud. " *'One. Check electrodes in fusion jar.'* "

"Fusion jar? Where . . . ?" Waving a long forefinger in front of him like a metal detector, Jonathan stooped to examine the lower shelf of the TASC cart. "Whoa! I can't believe this." His finger came to rest on an appliance topped by a plastic jar, three quarters full of a clear liquid. "I think he was trying to use this for cold fusion."

"That's our blender," exclaimed Emily.

"Grandpa used it in his time machine?" Matt started to laugh.

But Jonathan didn't even smile. "It could supply the energy you'd need, all right," he muttered. He squinted at the tubes and wires sticking out of the top of the blender, touching them gently here and there. He began to hum tunelessly as he always did when he was thinking hard. "What's the next step?" he asked Emily.

" *Two. Adjust resonator for distance of traveler from lens.'* " Emily glanced up from the notes to the pink crystal fastened over the projector on the top shelf. " *'Traveler,'* " she repeated. She took a deep breath, then burst out. "Listen! I get dibs on trying it first, okay? Where do I sit?"

Matt laughed again. "Em," he began.

But Jonathan, peering at the connections to the projector, interrupted. "You don't *sit* anywhere," he said without looking up. "You don't ride the TASC like a motorcycle, because *it* doesn't go anywhere. You stand in front of this." He pointed to the lens with the pink crystal fastened over it. "It's a simple process of projection."

"Okay, whatever," said Emily. "I just want to be first."

Jonathan gave a little laugh. "You don't have to go one at a time, either."

17

Matt stared at his friend. He wasn't surprised at the way Emily was talking, but Jonathan — "Don't you understand what this is all about, man? Grandpa wanted so bad to get back to the *Titanic* and save it, he convinced himself he could."

Jonathan, studying some tubing that led from one shelf to the next, didn't answer.

Matt laughed uneasily. "Hey. Don't tell me you think this crazy invention, this TASC, is going to work?"

"Probably not," agreed Jonathan. He turned to Emily. "What's number three in those notes?"

"Probably not?" repeated Matt. From Jonathan, that meant he thought it really might work. "But — What about what you said, about getting squished to a pulp in the space-time fabric?"

"Oh, that's just a theory I heard." Jonathan waved a hand, as if it were nothing to worry about. "This gadget doesn't have anything to do with black holes. It's a simple matter of resonance, and regrouping molecules. *If* it works. Big if."

But it *might* work, thought Matt. If his great-grandfather hadn't broken his leg, and if the TASC had worked for him, Grandpa Frank would be on the *Titanic* right now. A wave of excitement surged through Matt. What if he *could* do something for Grandpa Frank, after all?

Jonathan had fetched a screwdriver and was opening the back of the projector. Emily watched, scuffing one foot on the cement floor.

Matt cleared his throat. "Listen. Before you take the whole thing apart, we should get it out of here."

"You're right." Emily turned to Matt in alarm. "What if Mrs. Wilson comes out and makes us leave?"

"So let's take the thing" — somehow Matt didn't want to say what it was supposed to be — "to our house."

Jonathan nodded, although he looked sorry to have to stop working on the TASC for even a little while. "If it did work, we'd have to use it today — the date is important. Something to do with the resonance. Yeah, let's get this baby out of here."

"Yeah!" Smiling one of her big, toothy smiles, Emily popped the gray barbecue cover back over the invention. She and Jonathan began rolling the cart toward the front of the garage. Matt kicked cartons out of the way of the cart's squeaky little wheels and pushed up the big garage door.

But as Jonathan guided the cart down the driveway, Matt wondered what had come over him. In the spring sunshine, the lumpy thing hidden by the barbecue cover looked ridiculous. Jonathan couldn't seriously think it might work! He just wanted to fiddle with it because he loved fiddling with machines.

Still, Matt didn't quite want to say this aloud. He grasped one side of the TASC cart to steady it. Jonathan took hold of the other side. Emily tucked the clipboard under her arm and began pulling from the front. Together they trundled the wobbling, squeaking contraption along the sidewalk.

As they rolled the TASC through Grandpa Frank's neighborhood, Emily spoke up. "I do have first dibs, right? When we try it out?"

Jonathan, staring into space, took a moment to come out of his thoughts. Before he could answer, Matt said, "Give it up, Em. In the first place, it's not going to work. In the second place, if anybody should travel back to the *Titanic*, it's me. I know how to save the ship."

"To save — " Emily's light blue eyes squinted at him. Then she shouted, "Yes! We could really, actually do that for Grandpa! We could save the *Titanic*, like he wanted to do." She flashed Matt a grin. "But I'm going, too."

Stopping in the middle of the sidewalk, Jonathan stared down at them from his lanky height. "You guys have lost it," he said. "In the first place, quit arguing about who goes first. I told you, we could all go at the same time. In the second place, what we're trying to do here" — he patted the cover of Grandpa Frank's invention — "is achieve time travel. *Time travel!* If we somehow manage to just get to the *Titanic* and back, that would be the biggest breakthrough in scientific history. We can't tack another impossible project on top of that."

"This is Grandpa Frank's machine," said Emily sharply. "We have to use it the way he wanted to."

"Yeah, and he didn't build it for scientific history, man," said Matt. "He built it to go back to the *Titanic* and stop it from sinking."

"Or else I won't read any more notes," added Emily.

Jonathan drew back from their fierce stares. "Okay, okay!" He helped Matt lift the TASC cart over a ridge in the sidewalk. "Mission Impossible it is. Not that the thing's going to work, anyway."

"Don't talk like that," snapped Emily. "We have to think it *is* going to work, and then it will."

Matt smiled at his younger sister. That was the way Emily's soccer coach talked. Pep talks helped to win soccer games, but maybe not to make a time machine work.

Matt thought he was more realistic than Emily, but he couldn't keep his mind from circling back to the big WHAT IF. What if his great-grandfather's invention did work? What if the past *wasn't* over and done with, if it was still sitting back there somewhere? What if April 14, 1912, was a place you could go to?

Matt had a vision of himself like Superman, leaping back across decades. Pushing the forty-six-thousand-ton *Titanic* away from the fatal iceberg with one hand.

Of course that was ridiculous. But if Grandpa Frank thought *he* had a chance of saving the *Titanic*, why couldn't Matt? "It's not such an impossible mission," he said out loud. "There's a bunch of different ways the *Titanic* could have been saved. All the 'if onlys.' "

"What do you mean, 'if onlys'?" asked Emily.

"I mean, all the things that went wrong on the *Titanic*," said Matt. "Like, the ship might not have sunk *if only* the lookouts had had binoculars, *if only* the radio operators had given the officers all the ice warnings, *if only* the rich passengers had gotten scared and kicked up a fuss. . . ."

"Right now," interrupted Jonathan, "the big 'if only' is *if only* the TASC works. And if only we can get it to work this afternoon."

"Why? What happens if you don't get it to work until tomorrow?" asked Emily.

"He means we'd have to wait another year to travel to the *Titanic*." Matt bent over the TASC cart, rattling it along faster. Emily's mouth thinned out to a line as she hurried backward, pulling the cart.

It was several blocks from the neighborhood where Grandpa Frank lived to Matt and Emily's house in a new development. No one said anything until they'd rolled Grandpa Frank's invention across the last street.

"The deli, finally," remarked Jonathan. The Pinesbridge Delicatessen was on the corner of Matt and Emily's street. Now it was only a short stretch down a winding hill to the Cowens' split-level house.

From the Cowens' driveway, they trundled the top-heavy TASC over the flagstone walk to the front door ("You guys are stepping on daffodils," Emily pointed out) and hauled it up the half-flight of stairs to the hall. "We'd better put this thing in my room," panted Matt. "Just in case we aren't . . . *through* before Mom or Dad gets home."

In Matt's room, Jonathan wiped his forehead with the bottom of his Scorpion T-shirt. He whipped the cover off the TASC. "Okay! Let's take a look at this baby."

Emily flipped through the notes on the clipboard. "The next part is diagrams — I'll just read the titles for you. This one is *'Resonator,'* this is *'Projector'* . . ."

While Matt and Emily watched, Jonathan

poked and squinted at the various machines and instruments on the TASC cart, checking them against the diagrams on the lined yellow paper. He hummed and muttered under his breath. Finally he straightened his lanky frame and announced, "It's all set. Mr. Kenny had it basically ready to go. But I still don't see how — "

"One more thing in the notes." Emily turned the page on the clipboard. "It says, *'Place photo of arrival site in projector.'* And then there's this diagram, *'Remote control.'* "

"Photo — uh-oh," said Jonathan. "It was probably a photo that Mr. Kenny was trying to get from the shoebox in the rafters."

" *'Photo of arrival site,'* " repeated Matt. He pulled a book on the *Titanic* from his bookcase and opened it to the pictures in the middle. "Why couldn't this be our arrival site?" He showed Jonathan and Emily a photo of the boat deck, the top level of the ship, in the part where second-class passengers took walks.

"All you need in the picture is an empty space to land in, right?" asked Emily.

Jonathan nodded slowly. "Put that in the projector, and she's ready to roll. No, wait a minute." Jonathan started to take Matt's posters down from one wall. "We need a big white space to project the picture on. And we need to move the bed, because we'll have to stand in just the right place, to fit in."

After the posters were unpinned and the bed pushed aside, Jonathan measured off the distance between the projector lens and the wall. He measured off another distance, about halfway between. Matt stuck down three lengths of tape on the carpet there. Emily plugged in a cord and flipped the projector switch.

Then Emily gasped. Matt caught his own breath. On the wall that had been covered with his posters, there was now one picture from floor to ceiling.

"Why is it pink?" asked Matt in a low voice.

"The rose quartz, remember?" Emily pointed to the crystal fastened over the projector lens.

Huge smokestacks reared up and out of sight at the top of the picture. Below the smokestacks, folded wooden deck chairs leaned against a wall. To the left, groups of passengers strolled past a row of lifeboats.

And in the foreground, a stretch of empty deck waited.

Matt felt his stomach drop. There it was, 1912 — a place you could go to. Only — he realized suddenly — not the way they were dressed. "Just in case this works, we should put our good clothes on," he said. "Em, you'd better wear your green velvet dress, and your black shoes. And do something with your hair."

"My Christmas dress, and those pinchy shoes?" Emily made a horrible face. "Why couldn't I just pretend I come from a foreign country where the girls wear sweatsuits?"

"No. Look, everyone on the *Titanic* was dressed up." Matt grabbed his book from the projector and showed her more pictures of passengers. "Jonathan and I have to dress up, too."

"We do?" Jonathan looked as disgusted as Emily.

"Don't you guys understand anything about history?" demanded Matt. "Nobody in 1912 dressed anything like this." He waved a hand from Emily's sweatsuit to Jonathan's Scorpion T-shirt. "If we look weird to the people on the *Titanic*, they'll never listen to us." Matt stopped. He was talking, he realized, as if they were really going to the year 1912. "I mean, on the tiny little chance that we get there . . . See?" He shoved the pictures under Jonathan's nose.

"Dorky," muttered Jonathan. But he switched off the projector and went home to get his sport jacket and tie. Emily put on the dark green velvet dress with the white lace collar and stuck a green bow in her hair.

"Perfect!" said Matt at the sight of his sister, dressed up for the first time since Christmas. "But you'd better get your coat. All the passengers in the pictures are wearing coats. Your good coat, not your parka." He got a sweater for himself, and one for Jonathan. Then he finished

26

knotting his tie and went to find the binoculars in the family room cupboard.

When they were gathered in Matt's room again, Jonathan switched the projector back on. The smokestacks and deck chairs leapt onto the wall. Emily knelt to plug in the heavy-duty yellow extension cord connected to the blender. The machine began to whir and bubble.

Jonathan picked up the remote control. "Okay, everyone stand on the tape."

Matt's stomach flipped. He'd thought he was hoping against hope that his great-grandfather's time travel invention would work. Now, he felt he'd rather jump out of an airplane than try out the TASC. "That thing couldn't really put us back in 1912."

Jonathan shrugged. "It's a simple matter of — " His words ended in a croak, as if his throat were suddenly too dry to explain what it was a simple matter of.

"I think we should forget the whole deal," said Matt. "It's crazy, messing around with something that we don't even know — something that might — "

Emily didn't say anything. Under the green velvet bow, her red hair stood out from her head as if she were electrified. Her eyes had taken on an eerie color, like a reflection from an iceberg. She stepped into the pink light, onto a strip of tape. Behind, her shadow stepped into the picture from the *Titanic*.

Matt swallowed hard. One thing he knew for sure: He wasn't letting his sister try this without him, leaving him to explain things to their parents. He stepped onto the tape beside Emily, blinking into the pink light of the projector. Jonathan quickly took his place beside Matt.

"Stand absolutely still." Jonathan held up the remote control. "I'm going to do TRANSPORT." He pressed a button.

A high-pitched hum, like a VCR rewinding, came from the TASC. "What's that weird tingling?" exclaimed Emily.

"It's a simple matter of disassembling our molecules and rearranging them in another spacetime," croaked Jonathan.

"You didn't tell us it would — " Matt started to shout.

But his voice faded away like a wisp of smoke. His whole body was falling apart. He wondered if this was how World War II soldiers felt, when they got blown up by a direct artillery hit. He was blind and deaf and helpless. A giant vacuum cleaner tube was sucking the scrambled pieces of him back, back, back.

This is my fault, thought Matt. I shouldn't have let Jonathan . . . I shouldn't have let Emily . . .

3.
Iceberg Warnings

Jonathan *fwooped* through nothingness like a bunch of Lego pieces sucked into a jet engine. Even his mind felt jumbled up. Part of it was thinking, This is just the way you'd expect to feel, traveling through time. Another part screamed a terrified, drawn-out *Aagh*! He'd screamed inside like that once before: the time he went on the Boomerang, the scariest roller coaster ride in the world. Only now there was no one to stop the machinery before it killed him.

Hey, it *was* stopping. He could see again. Jonathan was looking at a railing a few yards ahead of him. It was hazy, but getting thicker, and so were the foggy shapes of Matt and Emily beside him. He was tingling again — and now the tingling sensation was gone.

Something was still humming, but not the TASC. This hum was deeper, far underneath the boards they stood on. The light in Jonathan's eyes was bright, but it wasn't pink. A sea breeze lifted the hair on his forehead.

Jonathan shut his eyes against the sunlight glaring off the ocean. He blinked them several times, just for the pleasure of being able to. Then he squinted over the railing and past the end of a lower deck.

There was a flat blue glittering expanse, broken only by a white trail — the ship's wake. "We made it!" he exclaimed.

"We made it, we made it!" shouted Matt and Emily. The three kids capered around each other, slapping hands in high-fives. Matt's binoculars bounced on his chest, and Emily's red hair blew into her mouth and eyes. They couldn't stop laughing.

This was better than the most fantastic adventures Jonathan had ever dreamed of. Better than a trip to Mars, better than exploring a deep ocean trench. He, Jonathan Schultz, had succeeded in transporting the three of them to April 14, 1912!

"Yeah!" Matt's face was red from laughing. "We did it! Everybody okay?"

Emily was grinning as if she had seventy-two teeth. She pulled a strand of hair from her mouth. "Let's go find Grandpa," she said breathlessly.

"What!" Jonathan came down to earth suddenly. "You can't do that."

"I don't see why not," said Matt, "but we can't spend much time down in third class. That's where he is, you know, with all the other immigrants."

"Are you — " Jonathan was so horrified that he choked on his words. "Don't you know that — Are you guys crazy? You can't go see your great-grandfather!"

"Shh," said Matt. He nodded toward a group of passengers, a family, strolling past. They wore long coats, and you could barely see their faces between their scarves and their hats. They all stared at the kids.

"I'm telling you," Jonathan went on in a desperate whisper, "don't go near your great-grandfather. You could change your own lives! You might never be born!"

"Okay, okay," said Matt. "But I think you watch too many science fiction movies."

Emily looked disappointed, but she shrugged. She glanced toward the family group, who had paused at the railing on the back of the deck. "Those people are still watching us."

"Yeah, we'd better split up," said Matt. "In fact," he went on eagerly, "that's the best way to handle the mission, to cover the 'if onlys.' Listen, here's the deal." His square chin lifted. He pulled at Jonathan's and Emily's sleeves to draw them into a huddle, as if it were understood that he was the leader.

"Hold it." Jonathan was still worried that they might accidentally change things just by being here in 1912. "I'm not sure we should be here at all," he began.

"Well, we are," said Matt impatiently.

"So let's go for it!" chimed in Emily.

"*As* I was saying," Matt started in again. Under his sandy brown hair, ruffled by the breeze, his face glowed. "I'm going to the bridge to talk to the officers. Then I'll find the lookout and give him these." He patted the binoculars hanging from his neck.

Jonathan wanted to explain more about how changing the past might ruin their present. But Matt rushed on, talking like a squad leader handing out assignments. "Schultz," he told Jonathan, "you should go to the wireless room and talk to the radio operators. Make sure they get all the ice warnings to the bridge. Then, if you have time, go down to the engine rooms."

"What about me?" asked Emily.

But Matt was so full of admiration for his master plan that he didn't seem to hear his sister. "If by some chance I don't get the officers to slow the *Titanic* down," he explained to Jonathan, "you can figure out how to stop the engines before the ship hits the iceberg! See?"

"I'm not sure it'll be such a piece of cake," Jonathan muttered.

Matt glanced over his shoulder at a man in a

dark uniform, carrying a steamer blanket over one arm. "That steward is watching us. Let's go. Em, I'll explain your part on the way to the bridge. Let's say we all meet at midnight, right here. We should have plenty of time, because the *Titanic* didn't hit the iceberg until eleven-forty at night."

"Whoa!" Jonathan was hit with a new worry. "Meet at *midnight*? What if we *can't* stop the accident from happening? We might go down with — "

"We *are* going to stop it," interrupted Emily. "We know all the if-onlys."

"Relax, Schultz," Matt told Jonathan. "Whatever happens, midnight is plenty of time — the *Titanic* took more than two hours to sink." He started around the deck chairs, toward the right side of the ship.

Emily exclaimed sharply, "Just a minute!" She hurried after her brother, her patent leather shoes slapping the deck.

"Hey, hold it!" Jonathan leapt after Matt, too. "Where *is* the wireless room?"

"Port and forward." Matt waved toward the opposite side of the ship. "Just before the bridge, in with the officers' quarters."

Jonathan fell back, staring after Matt and Emily as they disappeared around a smoke-stack. Feeling the eyes of the steward and the passengers on him, he dropped the TASC control into his pants pocket. He edged his way past another group of passengers, ducking under some of the lines that ran from a lifeboat up to the smokestack.

On Jonathan's left, three more lifeboats were lined up along the railing. To his right, amidships, there was a platform edged by a railing and topped by a low white building. The last of the four massive smokestacks towered above all. Ahead, the deck stretched the length of several blocks.

As he walked on past the lifeboats, Jonathan decided it was too late to worry about changing the past. Their whole reason for coming, after all, was to save the *Titanic*. And that would *really* change the past. He stepped up to the railing and leaned over curiously. Whoa! That was a long drop, down to where waves swished against the hull. Maybe six stories.

Turning away from the railing, Jonathan took a deep breath, pulled himself up to his full skinny height, and straightened his shoulders. Okay, he had a mission here: *If only the wireless operators had given the officers all the iceberg warnings*. That would be a simple matter. Jonathan could offer to carry the messages to the bridge himself, if the operators were too busy.

Walking in long strides, Jonathan let himself through a wire gate labeled ENGINEERS' PROM-

ENADE, then another gate marked FIRST CLASS ONLY. Ahead of him on the right was a building with tall arched windows, and a sign, FIRST CLASS ENTRANCE. There was a small door farther on, opposite the next set of lifeboats. Did it lead to the wireless room?

Jonathan stopped in front of the small door and raised his eyes. Aha! Wires, running down to the roof. They connected to more wires overhead — a radio antenna, if he wasn't mistaken, running the length of the deck. The radio or wireless room ought to be in this building.

Inside, a couple of turns in the hall took Jonathan to a closed door. He could hear a syncopated rhythm tapping on the other side: *dit-dit-da-dit*. Morse code — that was the way they sent radio messages in the early days. Each group of dashes and dots, tapped out with a telegraph key, stood for a different letter or number.

Jonathan eased the door open. "I think you've got it, Jack," said a boyish voice.

"Hang it! Now I've lost it again," said a second voice.

Jonathan poked his head in the doorway. A young man with a round-cheeked face sat at a table, hunched over a telegraph key. The wireless equipment, including a rivet-studded metal box with knobs on the top and sides, and a large spool of wire fixed sideways on a stand, took up most of the table. More equipment, encased in metal with dangling wires, was mounted on the wall behind it.

The operator fiddled with knobs and wires. He touched his headset, a headband around his forehead with bulky earphones attached to each side. He fiddled some more.

Another young man, darker than the first, leaned on the table beside him and watched intently. Like the seated wireless operator, he wore a dark wool uniform with a double-breasted jacket. The scene reminded Jonathan of something very familiar, he couldn't think what.

The seated man tapped at a brass lever with the tips of his fingers. Blue sparks flashed under his hand.

"Whew!" exclaimed the man leaning over him. "Well done, Jack. Now we can dig into that pile of messages to send."

A tube beside the table coughed and spat out a can. "Another message for the pile," groaned Jack, opening the can. "Very important greetings from Auntie Mabel to the folks back home."

"I'll take over for a while, if you like," offered the other. He glanced around, and his dark eyebrows shot up as he noticed Jonathan in the doorway. "Hello! It's a beanpole lad who wants to be a Sparks when he grows up."

"Send him away, Harold." Jack worked at the telegraph key, not looking up. "Tell him it's fourteen-hour shifts for thirty dollars a month, and no gratitude."

"*Twenty* dollars a month for the junior operator," corrected Harold, jerking his thumb at himself.

In spite of their grumbling, Jonathan could see that Jack and Harold loved being wireless operators. They looked as pleased with themselves as the computer hackers he knew. Feeling at home, Jonathan stepped through the doorway and pulled up a chair.

Jack and Harold went on with their work, as if they were used to boys hanging around the wireless room to watch. After a few minutes, Jonathan saw a way he could help. As the tube coughed out new messages, he took the slips of paper from the cans, smoothed them out, and added them to the pile. The tube must work on compressed air, he figured. The *fwoop* it made reminded him of his own recent journey through time and space.

Harold noticed Jonathan's help with an approving nod. "The job could be worse," he said. "At least the *Titanic* has the best wireless set afloat. A five-kilowatt transmitter, with a four-hundred-mile range in the daytime and up to three thousand miles at night."

Jonathan tried to look properly impressed. Obviously the *Titanic* was equipped with the most up-to-date radio technology — for 1912.

"And of course most ships can't keep a twenty-four-hour wireless watch, like we do, because they've only got one operator," added Jack.

"And no one to bring the poor fellow a sandwich as he slaves away," said Harold. "Look here, Slim," he told Jonathan, "want to make yourself useful? Run down to the galley and ask for a very large plate of sandwiches for Mr. Phillips and Mr. Bride. A few for yourself, as well," he added with a smile.

"Okay, sure!" Jonathan swung out of the wireless room, pleased with his progress. Jack and Harold were going to let him hang around. They'd chat about this and that, and sooner or later Jonathan would get a chance to bring up the subject of iceberg warnings.

Near the first-class entrance, Jonathan got directions to the *Titanic*'s galley from a passing steward. A short while later he climbed back up the four flights of stairs, balancing a tray with a pile of ham sandwiches and a pot of tea. Not a drop of the tea had spilled, he noticed. This ship wasn't pitching and rolling, like the few boats he'd been on. Only the deep vibration of the engines and the creaking of wood hinted that this was an ocean liner, not a hotel.

It was almost dark outside by the time Jonathan returned to the wireless room. Jack and Harold pounced on the supper tray. Harold found an extra mug for Jonathan and motioned for him to help himself to sandwiches and tea. Jonathan gratefully obeyed.

"I'll tell you what you ought to do in a few years, if you still want to be a Sparks," Harold told Jonathan between bites. "You ought to go to a School of Telegraphy, as I did. Of course you could learn the trade on your own, but the steamship companies like to see a certificate."

Jonathan nodded, his mouth full. But he wasn't really listening. He was only thinking how glad he was to be fed. Were Matt or Emily getting anything to eat? If they'd thought the TASC was actually going to work, they could have planned this part more carefully, so they wouldn't miss dinner.

Harold and Jack split the last sandwich and then became absorbed in their work. Jonathan settled himself in a corner to watch and listen. For something to do, he concentrated on the clicking of the telegraph key and tried to decode the outgoing messages.

Jonathan knew Morse code pretty well. He'd tried to get Matt to learn the code, too, so they could send messages back and forth. It would have been fun to tap out smart remarks with a pencil in history class. But Matt had lost interest after memorizing only half the Morse alphabet.

Now, as Jonathan listened to the *dit-da-dit-dit* with his eyes closed, bits of the messages Jack was tapping out started to come clear. RESERVE DOUBLE ROOM MR. & MRS. . . . A message to a hotel in New York. BUY 2000 SHARES RAND . . . That must be about the stock market.

Finally Harold yawned an enormous yawn. Jack told him, "Go on, turn in. I don't fancy having to lug you to bed when you keel over."

"In a minute," said Harold. He stretched and glanced at the clock. "It's nighttime at last. *Now* we'll get Cape Race loud and clear."

"Cape Race — is that another ship?" asked Jonathan.

"Cape Race, Newfoundland," explained Harold. "It's the nearest transmitter on land. By the way, do you know Morse code? I thought I saw you tapping it out with your finger." He lifted the headset from his head. "Here, have a listen. But hand it over if a message starts coming in."

For a few minutes there was only a faint crackling. Jonathan picked up a pencil and doodled a ship with four smokestacks. He was just drawing a spiral of smoke out of the forward smokestack when an incoming message started to spell itself out in *dits* through the earphones. He wrote it down in block letters: THREE LARGE BERGS . . .

"Is that a message?" Harold lifted the headset

off Jonathan and nudged him out of the chair. He listened, then finished printing the message: THREE LARGE BERGS FIVE MILES TO SOUTHWARD OF US.

"Who's that?" asked Jack casually. "Oh, the *Californian*."

Jonathan's heart skipped a beat. "Bergs? *Ice*-bergs?" He looked from Jack to Harold. "Aren't you going to tell the captain?"

Jack gave him an odd look. "It's not a message to us, you know. It's to the *Antillian,* another ship. We only overheard it."

Harold stood up, handing the headset to Jack. "Oh, I'll give the message to someone on the bridge. They don't much care, though — they just tack it up on the charts."

Jonathan's mouth was dry. He couldn't believe he'd been sitting around, chatting and eating sandwiches, as if he had all the time in the world. He was on a ship steaming straight into an ice field! "But this might be *serious*. If the *Titanic* hit an iceberg, I mean."

On his way out the door, Harold slapped Jonathan on the shoulder. "You're right, Slim! It would be most serious — for the iceberg." His chuckle faded away outside.

A chill crept over Jonathan, although the wireless cabin was warm. He'd almost forgotten that he was on the *Titanic*, with only a few hours left before the collision.

"An iceberg isn't a big icicle, you know!" Jonathan spoke to Jack in a low, intense voice. "It's a chunk of a *glacier*. That means it's been squeezing together for thousands of years until the ice is as hard as diamonds. It can slice through steel like — "

The wireless operator made a shooing motion with his left hand. He didn't look up, but the meaning was clear: Shut up, kid. His right hand tapped the telegraph key in an expert flutter.

Jonathan leaned back in his chair and silently spelled out the message Jack was sending: POKER BUSINESS GOOD. AL.

Maybe I shouldn't be so upset, thought Jonathan. Maybe it was my question that got Harold to take the ice warning from the *Californian* to the bridge. If the officers did pay attention to that warning, then — mission accomplished.

Harold reappeared. "Mind if I turn in now, Jack?" He gave another huge yawn. "I'm not like you — I can't work on until I drop dead."

Without looking around, Jack turned over the message on the top of the pile and picked up the next one. "That's why you're only Second Wireless Operator," he said with a grin. "Go on, get some sleep. You've got until two A.M."

"No, I'll wake up sooner than that," Harold assured him. "Good night, Slim," he said to Jonathan.

But before Harold could disappear behind the

green curtain at the back of the room, Jonathan jumped up. "Hey, wait. What did they say on the bridge, when you gave them the iceberg warning?"

Harold paused with a hand on the curtain. "Why, nothing. They never say anything. Anyway, we've given them three or four other ice warnings today. It's only one more of the same."

"But — " Jonathan stammered. "If there're so many warnings, doesn't that mean they should be seriously worried? You should make them — You should tell them — "

Harold interrupted with a short laugh. "You have some strange notions, boy. Wireless operators don't tell the officers anything. We send and receive — that's *our* business. They navigate — that's *their* business."

Jonathan had a sick feeling in his stomach. "But we're talking about a terrible accident, if — "

"I can't talk any more nonsense." Harold cut him off. "I'm beat." The junior wireless operator opened the door to the hall, motioning Jonathan out. "And Jack's got a backlog of messages to send — he doesn't want you pestering him." Harold added in a friendlier tone, "Drop in again tomorrow. You can have another go at the headset, if we're not too busy."

4.
The Heartbeat of the *Titanic*

There didn't seem to be anything Jonathan could do except follow the corridor back out to the boat deck. Outside, a million stars glittered in the black sky. Jonathan shivered and folded his arms. The temperature must have dropped several degrees since he'd carried the sandwiches up from the galley. Well, of course it was cold — these were iceberg waters.

Drop in again tomorrow, Harold had said. There might not be any tomorrow on the *Titanic*.

Jonathan peered forward, toward the bridge. Was Matt having any luck at getting the officers to worry about the icebergs ahead? Not from what Harold had said.

Shoving his hands into his pockets, Jonathan felt the TASC control. Maybe he'd been right in the first place, when he said it was too much to try to save the *Titanic*. Maybe he should find Matt and Emily and just get out of here, before . . .

But there *were* a few hours left, and Jonathan hadn't even tried his second mission. He glanced up at the sky, where a plume billowed from the forward smokestack. That smoke came from the furnaces far below, where steam drove the mighty engines of the *Titanic*.

If Jonathan left the *Titanic* now, he'd be letting Mr. Kenny down. The old man would never know it, but Jonathan would. Worse, Jonathan would be leaving Jack and Harold to go down with the ship. He couldn't do that. The wireless operators reminded him of the guys he liked to schmooze with through his computer, trading notes on science fiction.

Jonathan's teeth were chattering. He glanced up once more at the brilliant night sky, then headed down the nearest stairway. He ought to reach the engine rooms if he just kept going down, deck after deck after deck.

At each level, the giant heartbeat of the engines throbbed louder. Jonathan wondered exactly what he would do, once he got below. Of course Matt's general idea made sense: If the *Titanic* weren't going forward at 11:40 P.M., it couldn't crash into the iceberg.

So Jonathan was supposed to go down to the engine rooms, wait until shortly before the moment of collision, and then stop the ship. The question was, how? Matt had talked as if it were just a simple matter of stepping on the brakes.

Down on E deck, Jonathan noticed more passengers in the corridors. These people had on old, worn clothes. This must be third-class space, where the immigrants from all different countries traveled, he thought as he climbed down still another stairway.

Jonathan doubted that any of these passengers would report him to a steward. But just in case, he looked carefully up and down the corridor on F deck before he slipped through a door marked CREW ONLY. Aha — this was the way to the deck below.

Climbing down the steep cast-iron steps, Jonathan began to sweat. He took off his jacket and sweater and bundled them under his arm. The railing hummed in his hands. At the foot of the steps, the steel floor shook under his feet.

Jonathan stepped cautiously into a space murky with smoke. Men with blackened faces shoveled coal into open furnaces. Beside the gigantic boilers that crowded the belly of the ship, the men stoking the furnaces seemed tiny, like mice tending whales.

The furnaces roared. Somewhere down here, the engines beat out a thunderous rhythm. Through a steel doorway Jonathan glimpsed more furnaces, more stokers shoveling. He couldn't see how far the chain of boiler rooms went on.

Where were the engine rooms? If Jonathan

got a look at the engines, maybe he could figure out how to stop them.

Jonathan began to sneak around the swollen hulks of the boilers. He took his time, keeping to the shadows, moving when no one was looking his way. At least he didn't have to worry about anyone hearing his footsteps over the din of the furnaces and the engines.

Finally Jonathan found himself outside the last boiler room. A monster machine rose several stories above him, shaking the bulkhead as its pistons churned. This was it — the heartbeat of the *Titanic*.

Matt is crazy, thought Jonathan. "Stop the engines" — yeah. The ship wasn't exactly like a car, where you could just lift the hood and cut a fan belt.

As Jonathan stared up at the giant engine, a man appeared in the gloom. He was walking straight toward Jonathan. As if he'd read Jonathan's mind and knew he was planning to stop the engine.

His heart pounding, Jonathan ducked back into the boiler room. An extra shovel lay beside the coal bunker. Without stopping to think it over, Jonathan stuffed his coat and sweater into a corner, yanked off his clip-on tie, and rolled up his sleeves. He grabbed the shovel and started stoking the furnace.

A moment later, he glimpsed a man in uni-

47

form walking by behind him. Jonathan bent his head over the shovel, thankful for the smoke and gloom. In the old days, didn't they used to punish kids like him as if they were adults? They might think he was a terrorist or something.

After a few minutes of shoveling, sweat was running down Jonathan's face, and his shoulders began to ache. He slowed down, but he didn't dare stop. How did the stokers shovel for hours on end without dropping dead?

Jonathan wished he knew how Matt and Emily were doing with their missions. If they succeeded, how could he tell — would he hear the engines slowing down? He wouldn't mind, now, if someone else had the honor of saving the *Titanic*. As long as they did it quickly.

Jonathan jabbed his shovel into the pile of coal, heaved the shovelful into the furnace. Jab, heave. Jab, heave. His arms hurt. It seemed like an eternity before the head stoker shouted, "Rest your shovels, boys!"

The man next to Jonathan at the furnace offered him a mug of tea, and they sat down on overturned buckets. "Nice clean work, eh?" the man remarked.

Jonathan, using his sleeve to wipe coal dust and sweat from his face, thought the stoker must be kidding. But a man nearby spoke up in agreement. "The *Titanic*'s a real beauty. A lucky day for us when we signed on her. Not like stoking on an old ship, slogging our guts out and nearly roasted with the heat."

Jonathan began to relax. Since the *Titanic* was brand-new, maybe the crew didn't know each other very well — not well enough to spot a face that didn't belong. Especially when all the faces were streaked with soot. After the stokers went back to work, maybe Jonathan could sneak back to the engine room.

Then a heavy hand fell on Jonathan's shoulder. He froze. A man in uniform — he must be an engineer — was scowling down at him.

"What're you doing here?" bellowed the engineer above the noise of the furnace. He yanked Jonathan to his feet. "Do you speak English? Fred" — he motioned to a man in shirtsleeves, the head stoker — "says you're not a stoker."

"No more than 'e is," said Fred. " 'E 'andles 'is shovel like a blooming teaspoon. Maybe 'e's an anarchist, going to set off a bomb down here and blow us all to Kingdom Come."

This was so close to what Jonathan really planned that he started shaking. "I'm sorry, sir," he told the engineer. His voice came out in a squeak. "I — I wasn't sure you'd let me look around. I just wanted to see — " He stopped, not daring to say he wanted to see the engines.

"Why, he's a Yank." The engineer's face relaxed, and he looked as if he was trying not to smile.

"And only a boy," added Fred, grinning good-naturedly. "My mistake. 'E's earned 'imself a look around, wouldn't you say, Mr. Hesketh?"

"Come along, then," said Engineer Hesketh, nodding toward the doorway. "Fred and I will give you a tour."

Relieved, Jonathan picked up his jacket and sweater and followed Hesketh and Fred into the next boiler room. At least he wasn't going to be thrown in the brig. And maybe this was his chance to find out how to stop the ship.

"You know," said Hesketh to Jonathan, "even if some desperate fellow did set off a bomb down here, and blasted a hole in the hull, that wouldn't sink *this* ship."

"That's right," agreed Fred. "That there door would slam down." He jerked a blackened thumb at the doorway they'd just stepped through. "And that there door would slam down. And she'd be tight as tight again."

Jonathan looked back and forth from the doorway at one end of the boiler room to the other. That made sense. But it wasn't the way it had happened — was *going* to happen, fairly soon. Because the *Titanic hadn't* been sealed tight. She had filled up with water and sunk.

Jonathan stared through the smoke at the riveted steel wall of the ship. The Atlantic Ocean was just on the other side of that metal skin.

What time was it by now? He forced back an impulse to run up the nearest ladder.

Hesketh and Fred strolled on into the next boiler room. Hesketh was shouting, above the roar and throb, that the *Titanic* was a triple-screw steamship. That meant it had three propellers.

Jonathan followed the engineer and the head stoker, although he knew they were leading him toward the bow of the ship. With every step, he was farther from the engines he had to stop. How was he going to find out what he needed to know?

Maybe the best way was just to ask. "So, Mr. Hesketh," he said conversationally, "how would you stop this ship? I mean, if you had to stop quickly."

The engineer smiled. "She couldn't stop *quickly*, not at the speed we're going. We're up to twenty-four knots tonight, and this old girl" — he patted a steel door frame fondly — "weighs in at forty-six thousand tons."

Twenty-four knots, thought Jonathan. A knot was a little over a mile per hour, so say the ship was steaming along at twenty-eight miles per hour. That didn't seem too fast. It wouldn't be fast, if they were driving a car on a highway. But if you were steering a ship the size of a small town through a sea full of icebergs, twenty-eight miles per hour was a daredevil speed.

51

He'd have to stop the *Titanic* well before she was due to hit the iceberg. Jonathan wondered if there was some lever or button in the engine room — unfortunately at the other end of this deck — that would do the trick. "But how would they stop the ship?" he asked Fred.

"Well, first we'd get the order from the bridge, full speed astern," explained the head stoker. "The telegraph bells would ring your ears off. And see that red light above the door?" He pointed up to where a white light shone beside an unlit red one. "The red light would flash. The white light, now, that means 'full speed ahead.'"

"And then in the engine room, how would they stop the propellers?" persisted Jonathan.

"We don't just stop them; we reverse them," corrected Engineer Hesketh. "Except for the center propeller, since that works off the turbine."

"Meanwhile," Fred put in, "we stokers jump to damp the fires, to keep the steam down."

Jonathan didn't see how he was going to do all this. How could he possibly find out exactly what they did in the engine rooms to control the propellers, and then do it without anyone noticing and stopping him, and at the same time get the stokers to damp the fires? But wait — he *wouldn't* have to do all that, if he could somehow make the telegraph bells ring and the red light flash. But the officers did that from up on the bridge, not down here.

"Do you know what time it is?" he asked Fred. "I have an — um — appointment up on the boat deck." He pulled on his sweater and jacket.

Fred shrugged. "After eleven, anyway. Near the end of my shift, which I'm 'appy to say."

After eleven! How had Jonathan lost track of time so badly? The *Titanic* was going to hit the iceberg at 11:40. He had to leave for the bridge right now.

5.
First Class

Emily hurried after her brother, away from the spot where they'd landed on the *Titanic*. The afternoon sun shone in her face and glanced off the dazzling white, newly painted ship, making her squint.

"Matt." Emily grabbed his sleeve. "Listen, never mind explaining my part to me."

Matt halted beside a row of lifeboats, a puzzled expression on his face. His gray-blue eyes under level brows made him look fair-minded, which he actually was most of the time. But sometimes he just didn't get it.

"I know what I'm going to do," Emily told him.

"But I thought you could take the binoculars to — "

"No, you can do that." Emily cut him off. "I'm going to find some of those rich passengers you were talking about." As Matt gazed at her doubtfully, she added, "Didn't you say if they got scared about icebergs, they could make the captain slow the ship down?"

"Ye-es," admitted Matt. "If you could make them pay attention to you. You'd have to go to the first-class section of the ship, where the rich passengers hang out."

"Fine," said Emily. "Where is the first-class section?"

Matt started off again. "It's on the way to the bridge — I'll show you."

Emily fell into step with her brother. Matt could be so annoying, she thought, when he got that mature and noble expression on his face. As if he would try to be patient and tactful, but he knew what was best.

Matt opened a gate, stepped through, and latched it behind Emily. "Only you have to understand, Em," he went on, "this is a different time in history. You can't just wear the right clothes — you have to act right, too. People in nineteen-twelve expected kids to be super-polite."

Emily knew what he was thinking, but she said coldly, "So?"

"So, you can't just go blurting out whatever pops into your head. They'll think you're a brat."

"I know how to be polite, jerk," snapped Emily. To prove it, she smiled and nodded graciously at a couple strolling toward them.

There were only a few passengers on the starboard deck, all of them wrapped in coats and hats and scarves. Emily was glad she'd worn her coat, but she wished she'd put on tights, too. The breeze nipped her bare legs, and there wasn't much warmth in the bright sunlight.

They walked on and on, past more lifeboats, past two more smokestacks. "There's the gym," remarked Matt, nodding toward an open door. Emily glimpsed a rowing machine and a pair of rings. "That means we should be almost to the first-class entrance."

"No kidding." Emily pointed past a row of tall arched windows, at the sign above a revolving door: FIRST CLASS ENTRANCE.

"Oh, yeah, there it is," said Matt. "Well, just go in and go down the Grand Staircase. It's all first class, down on A deck." He hesitated, studying Emily with a big-brother expression. "But try not to get anyone mad at you. Think before you — "

"Thanks, Matt," said Emily, super-politely. "Thank you *so* much. Bye-bye. See you at midnight." She pushed through the revolving door.

Inside, Emily forgot about Matt's annoying ways. She stopped and gaped. It was as if she'd stepped into a palace. She was at the top of a double staircase — this must be the Grand Staircase Matt had mentioned — curving gracefully down into a foyer. Above the staircase arched the dome of a skylight.

Someone brushed by Emily in a rustle of silk and a scent of roses. A woman with long, up-swept hair floated down the staircase with one gloved hand on the polished railing. She reached the foyer and glided under the crystal chande-lier.

What a killer costume, thought Emily. Except that little waist means she must be wearing a corset — ugh. And her hat's decorated with birds' wings — ugh.

Emily followed the elegant woman down the staircase, pausing to gaze at the clock on the landing where the two flights of stairs met. It was set in an arched niche, richly decorated, with a statue of a girl in filmy robes on each side. You had to look twice to see that it *was* a clock.

Down in the foyer, Emily stared around the spacious hall. There was a murmur of conver-sation from people standing in clusters among the carved pillars and the palm trees. All the women wore long dresses and gloves and big fancy hats decorated with flowers or feathers. All the men wore suits, and most of them wore hats.

There weren't many children, Emily no-ticed — only those two little boys in sailor suits, holding their nanny's hands. There were a lot of stewards in dark uniforms, bustling through the passengers, running errands. Somewhere violins were playing light, graceful music.

As she stared up at the skylight again, Emily's head swam. She lowered her head quickly and put her hands on her knees. She was having that green-faced feeling she remembered from her class's whale watch field trip.

"Is something the matter, miss?" A steward, an older man with a kindly face, had stopped beside her. He bent down politely, waiting for her answer.

"I'm fine . . . thanks," said Emily.

"Very good, miss," he said with a little bow. "I only wondered if you might be lost, or not feeling quite well."

"I do feel a little funny," Emily admitted. While her head was telling her that the *Titanic* was too big and steady to seem like a ship, her stomach was paying more attention to the vibration from the engines down below. Her stomach knew that this *was* a ship, just as much as the whale watch ship.

The steward looked concerned. "Perhaps a breath of fresh air?" He took her by the elbow and led her to a door, which opened onto an enclosed deck space.

Taking deep breaths, Emily walked carefully over to a deck chair and sat down with her feet up. Much better out here. She pulled a blanket up over her bare legs and leaned back.

She'd sit here just until she felt all right. Then she'd charge back inside and start meeting people.

After a few minutes of breathing carefully, Emily was beginning to feel better. She was about to get up, when she heard footsteps behind her. A woman said in a teasing voice, "Someone's been sitting in my chair! But it's not Goldilocks, because she's got red hair."

Emily sat up straight and looked around. A plump, middle-aged woman smiled down at her from under a big hat covered with roses. She wore a long coat draped with a fur scarf.

"Oh, I'm sorry!" said Emily. "I didn't know — "

"Never mind, dearie." The woman took a calling card from the back of the chair and handed it to Emily. Then she settled on the edge of a nearby chair, looking amused. "I did put my card on that chair. But only to please the stewards, because they think it's the thing to do."

Emily studied the calling card. *Mrs. J. Brown.* Be polite, Emily. Maybe this was exactly the rich person she was looking for. "It's nice of you not to get mad, Mrs. Brown. I'm Emily Cowen. I sat outside here because I was feeling queasy, but I'm better, now."

"Pleased to meet you, Emily Cowen," said Mrs. Brown. "Fresh air, that's the ticket," she went on with a vigorous nod. "Fresh air and exercise. Why don't you come for a turn around the deck with me?" Mrs. Brown held out her hand, and Emily slid eagerly out of the deck chair.

As they rounded the front end of the deck, the breeze whipped Emily's hair. She gazed out over the ship's bow. There was nothing in sight from horizon to horizon but water. The *Titanic* might be a huge ship, but it was just a speck in the middle of the ocean.

The view made Emily think of her mission. She was about to bring up the subject of icebergs when Mrs. Brown nudged her. "See the elegant gentleman with the young wife? That's Mr. John Jacob Astor."

Emily looked at the couple leaning against the railing, the water shimmering behind them. "He looks like a prince."

"Well, I guess he is a kind of prince — an American prince." Mrs. Brown smiled knowingly. "But of course it was his father who made his money, in the fur trade."

"What did you make *your* money in, Mrs. Brown?" asked Emily. Immediately she was sorry she'd asked. Maybe it was rude, just the kind of thing Matt had warned her against blurting out.

But Mrs. Brown only laughed. She tucked Emily's hand under her arm in a friendly way as they walked on. "Fair enough. No, I didn't come from money. I grew up in a log cabin. My husband, Jim, and I used to live in a shack next to our mine, near Denver. Then one day we struck it rich in gold. Overnight, we were millionaires! Don't that beat everything?"

"It does," agreed Emily. She laughed, too, pleased with the way things were going. Mrs. Brown was a millionaire. *And* she seemed like the kind of person who wouldn't be shy about speaking to the captain, if she thought he ought to slow the ship down.

But now Mrs. Brown was frowning at Emily's hand on her coat sleeve. "Tsk, tsk — you've come out without your gloves. Or your hat, for that matter. Do your folks know where you are?"

Emily hesitated just an instant. Of course her mother and father didn't know where she was at all. But that wasn't a good answer. "I'm — I'm traveling with my great-grandfather," she said. "But he's in his room — he's sick."

That was all true. No need to explain that her sick great-grandfather was eighty-some years in the future. Or that the great-grandfather on this ship was a little boy (probably perfectly well), traveling third class. Emily felt a pang — she wanted to see him. How did Jonathan know that they shouldn't?

61

"No one to play with, hm?" said Mrs. Brown sympathetically. "Never mind. Do you like bicycles, Emily?"

Emily gave her a startled glance. "Yes, but what do bicycles have to do with anything?"

Mrs. Brown smiled without answering. She towed Emily through a revolving door, back into the foyer. Up the Grand Staircase, out onto the boat deck, and back the way Emily and Matt had come. The Denver millionairess waved a hand toward an open door, from which came a clicking sound.

"Come right in!" A short, wiry man in a white sweater and pants jumped off the rowing machine he was working. "Good afternoon, Mrs. Brown." He gave Emily a friendly nod.

Emily looked curiously around at the workout equipment. It was old-fashioned but at the same time gleaming new. There was no one else in the gym.

"Good afternoon." Mrs. Brown swept across the room toward a couple of bicycles mounted on stands. "We wish to use the cycling equipment." Over her shoulder, she grinned at Emily. "I'll bet I can beat you!"

"No way!" Emily dashed after her. They jumped onto the bicycles and began pedaling furiously. In front of them, red and blue arrows on a big dial marked the "distance" they were riding.

Emily was good at sports, and she thought she'd win easily. But for a plump, middle-aged woman wearing a corset, Mrs. Brown was not in bad shape. By the time Mrs. Brown called out, "You win!" Emily had a stitch in her side.

They cycled along more calmly for a few moments, catching their breath. Fun was fun, thought Emily, but it was time to get down to business. "Mrs. Brown — do you ever think about the fact that the *Titanic* could hit an iceberg?"

"Hit an iceberg?" Mrs. Brown gave Emily a quizzical look. "Good gracious, child. Why borrow trouble?" She nodded toward a window. "Do you see any icebergs out there?"

"No," said Emily, "but can't you imagine how horrible it would be, if the ship crashed into this killer iceberg" — she took her hands off the handlebars to smack them together — "and started to sink, and you couldn't get to a lifeboat in — "

"Time for tea," interrupted Mrs. Brown. She reached over to give Emily's hand a pat. "When I find myself thinking dreary thoughts, I take myself in hand. I ask myself, 'Molly, when's the last time you had some grub?' And I answer myself, 'Why, Mrs. Brown, that's it — I haven't had a bite since luncheon.'"

Emily had to chuckle at the idea of Mrs. Brown taking herself in hand. Sliding off her bicycle, she decided to let the subject of icebergs go, for the moment. They'd have time to talk over tea.

The gym instructor seemed disappointed to see them leave. "Come back later," he urged. "Try our mechanical horses, or the camel — very good for the liver. And then cool off in the swimming pool on F deck."

Mrs. Brown paused outside the gym to pull a chain from under her coat. It ended in a gold watch, set with diamonds. "Teatime, just as I reckoned. Steer for the lounge!"

Mrs. Brown was something like a steamship herself, thought Emily. She let herself be towed back down the Grand Staircase, across the foyer, and along a corridor with oak-paneled walls. If Mrs. Brown took charge like this with everyone, she might be just the person to make the captain of the *Titanic* listen to warnings about icebergs.

The corridor ended in the first-class lounge. The walls and ceilings of this spacious room were decorated with carved and painted and gilded curlicues. At one end of the room, musicians were playing a waltz, the music merging with the clinking of teacups. Mrs. Brown and Emily settled near the crackling blaze of the fireplace. A waiter immediately appeared, and Mrs. Brown ordered their tea.

"If you want to worry," Mrs. Brown said to Emily as she poured the tea, "I'll give you something to worry about." She stirred plenty of lemon and sugar into Emily's cup. "What if you sank out of sight in this carpet, and no one heard you yelling for help?"

Emily laughed, although she was getting a little frustrated with Mrs. Brown's cheerfulness. Still, it felt good to slip off her tight patent leather shoes under the tea table and wiggle her toes into the thick, soft carpet. And she felt starved.

"Go on, dig in," said Mrs. Brown, pointing to the plate of buttered toast. "In Denver, we like children to eat hearty."

As Emily and her new friend dug in, Mrs. Brown kept up a running commentary on the other people in the lounge. "That young man with the clipped mustache, standing by the fireplace, that's Archie Butt. He's an aide to President Taft. Across the way, on the little sofa, the lady in the hat with the white plumes, that's a real live countess."

A woman in a hat with a net veil swept up to Mrs. Brown and greeted her in a foreign accent. As the two women chatted, Emily ate and drank and gazed around the lounge.

The drapes were green velvet, the chairs were green brocade. On the wall across the room there hung a gilt-framed portrait of a girl. Her face was very pale, almost white. She wore a green dress, and a green bow in her red hair.

No. Emily paused with a little iced cake halfway to her mouth. That wasn't a painting — it was a mirror. That girl who fit into this room so well was her.

Emily gulped and turned away from the mirror. She felt panicky, as if she were trapped in someone else's movie. She and Matt and Jonathan had made it to 1912. But even if they saved the *Titanic*, what if they never made it back to their own time?

6.
"Serious Damage
Is Impossible"

Mrs. Brown and the foreign woman were saying good-bye. *"Adieu,* Molly." The veiled woman pinched Emily's chin and swept away.

"Real nice, isn't she?" remarked Mrs. Brown. "You'd never know she was related to the Russian nobility. Not like some of these folks on board" — she nodded around the lounge — "who think they're too fine to say 'How d'ye do' to Jim Brown's wife."

Emily decided there were no polite words to explain how she felt about having her chin pinched. But never mind that, or whether the TASC would return her and Matt and Jonathan to their own time. Right now, she was on a mission for Grandpa.

Emily sat up straight and licked the icing from the corners of her mouth. "I was wondering, Mrs. Brown — do you know the captain?"

Mrs. Brown looked surprised at Emily's serious tone. "Why, sure, I know Captain Smith. The finest gentleman on board, for my money. And of course he makes it his business to know all the first-class passengers. We had a real nice chat on deck the other day."

Emily leaned over the tea tray and spoke in a low voice. "So, if you were really upset about something, he'd listen to you?"

"Now, what on earth would I be upset about?" Mrs. Brown was smiling but mystified. "Captain Smith runs a ship better 'n any on the high seas, they say. A lot of these folks" — she waved her hand around the first-class lounge — "booked on the *Titanic* just because Captain Smith was going to be in command."

"But you have to admit," pressed Emily, "if the ship ran into an iceberg, it would be a total disaster. And — "

"Icebergs again!" Mrs. Brown leaned back in her chair, flapping a hand at Emily's silly idea. "Have another cake. Have a currant scone."

"No, thank you," said Emily. To herself she said, Don't get mad. Keep on being super-polite. She has to listen.

"I want you to listen to me, child," said Mrs. Brown before Emily could speak again. "You're letting your imagination run away with you. Let's think about some facts. Ready?"

Emily bit her lip and nodded.

"Fact number one," said Mrs. Brown, ticking

it off on her forefinger. "The *Titanic* is the biggest ocean liner *in the whole world*. Why, it's like sailing on the Rock of Gibraltar. Fact number two: This ship is brand-new. Down to the last little bolt and rivet, brand-new. Fact number three" — she bent back another finger, sparkling with rings — "Captain Smith feels so sure there's no danger, he hasn't even held a lifeboat drill yet."

"No lifeboat drill?" repeated Emily, swallowing hard. "That's crazy. When we do fire drills at school, we have to practice and practice. Just to make the kids go out the door they're supposed to."

"Now that I think of it, there was a drill scheduled for this morning." Mrs. Brown grinned. "But they held a Sunday church service instead. *I'd* have had more fun at a lifeboat drill."

Emily struggled against losing her temper. Mrs. Brown's cheerfulness was beginning to seem stupid.

"Fact number four." Mrs. Brown went on to her little finger. "There's a whole lot of folks on board who know all about ships. If there was any danger, they'd have some notion of it."

"Who are they?" asked Emily hopefully. Maybe if Mrs. Brown wouldn't take her seriously, one of them would.

"Oh, there's Mr. J. Bruce Ismay, chairman of the White Star Line — that's this fleet, of course. He's a real stuffed shirt, but I guess he knows his business. He's making a pile of money at it. Then there's Mr. Thomas Andrews, managing director of the shipbuilding firm that built the *Titanic*."

Emily leaned forward to ask if Mrs. Brown would introduce her to these men. But just then, a bugle sounded at the door of the lounge. Brushing crumbs off her chest with her napkin, the Denver millionairess stood up. "There, they're tooting at us to go dress for dinner. You'd better run along, Emily."

Jumping up, Emily followed Mrs. Brown through the lounge. "Could I have dinner with you, then? My great-grandfather can't get to the dining room." That's an understatement, she thought.

Mrs. Brown, lifting her long skirts with one hand as she swept through the lounge, gave Emily a quizzical look. "What a funny little thing you are. *Children* don't get dressed for dinner and come to the dining room. They put on their nightdresses and go to bed." She paused in the corridor and studied Emily. "Is someone looking after you, with your great-grandpa sickly? You can just ask the stewards for anything, you know. They're real helpful."

"I'm fine," said Emily hastily. "My older brother's on board, too." She wondered briefly how far Matt had gotten with his mission.

They brushed through potted palms into the pillared foyer again, and Mrs. Brown patted Emily on the shoulder. "Look me up tomorrow morning, dearie. We'll go for a swim."

Tomorrow morning! The thought that she might be in 1912 tomorrow morning made Emily's stomach drop. Unless the three kids from the future could save the *Titanic*, Emily would either be in a lifeboat or . . . or going for a swim, although not the way Mrs. Brown meant.

"But, Mrs. Brown — " Emily stopped, realizing that the rich woman wasn't listening.

Mrs. Brown was gazing up the Grand Staircase, where two men were descending the right-hand flight of stairs. One of them was tall and lean, with an arrogant air to his handlebar mustache.

The other man, with a weathered face and a trim white beard, looked quietly confident. He wore an officer's cap trimmed with gold braid, and a long navy-blue jacket with gold braid on the sleeves and a double row of brass buttons. Captain Smith, thought Emily.

Mrs. Brown nudged Emily. "There's the captain now, with J. Bruce Ismay, chairman of the board of the White Star Line. Oh, Captain Smith." She stepped toward the white-bearded man with a smile and a little bow. "And Mr. Ismay."

The captain smiled and bowed back. "Mrs.

Brown." Mr. Ismay gave Mrs. Brown only the smallest nod.

Mr. Ismay seemed to want to move on, but Captain Smith turned to Emily. "Mrs. Brown, who is your young friend?"

"I'm Emily Cowen." Before Mrs. Brown could say anything, Emily spoke up, looking the captain in the eye. "There's something important I have to talk to you about. Sir," she added quickly.

Mr. Ismay gave a snort, but the captain kept his twinkling eyes on Emily. "And what exactly is that something important?"

"It's about the icebergs ahead!" Emily blurted. "If you don't slow the ship down — "

Captain Smith burst out laughing. "Another ice warning? You must have been in the wireless room this morning, my dear." He turned to Ismay. "Do you still have that message from the *Baltic*?"

The chairman of the White Star Line pulled a slip of paper from his coat pocket, and Captain Smith held it out for Emily to see. *Icebergs and large quantity of field ice today in latitude 41.51 north, longitude 49.52 west,* she read.

"You see, Emily," said Captain Smith with a reassuring smile, "I am already aware of what you wish to tell me." He patted her on the head. "Don't worry, my dear. You may have heard frightening tales about unfortunate happenings in past times, but to a ship of this construction, serious damage is impossible."

With a bow to Mrs. Brown, Captain Smith was off across the foyer. Emily clenched her teeth. She couldn't believe he'd patted her on the head.

"Now, you see how foolish you've been?" Mrs. Brown shook a finger at Emily. "Run along to your cabin, before your poor old great-grandpa wonders if you fell overboard." The Denver millionairess sailed off around the foot of the Grand Staircase.

What now? The dress-for-dinner bugle sounded again from the top of the stairs. In the domed skylight above the staircase, the sky had changed from blue to deep purple. Passengers drifted out of the foyer, and soon it was almost empty.

Emily had wasted a lot of time on Mrs. Brown. She had to meet someone else. What about the names Mrs. Brown had mentioned, people on board who "knew all about ships"?

One of them was Mr. Ismay, but he was a "stuffed shirt." Emily had just seen that for herself. Another name was Thomas Andrews. If his company had built the *Titanic*, he must have a good idea what would happen if the ship hit an iceberg.

Emily went up to one of the stewards hurrying through the lounge. "Excuse me, can you tell me where Mr. Thomas Andrews is?"

The steward looked surprised, but he said politely, "I imagine Mr. Andrews is in his stateroom, A-thirty-six. I was going there in a minute to help Mr. Andrews dress for dinner."

"I'd better hurry, then," said Emily.

"Mr. Andrews is a very busy man," warned the steward with a frown. But he explained to Emily how to find stateroom A-36.

Emily went back to the lounge, empty now except for waiters clearing the tea things. On the other side of the room, she found another corridor and followed it past a cloakroom. Then, in a smaller foyer around another staircase, there was a door on the right that said A-36 in brass.

Emily had to knock twice before a man's voice called, "Come in." She stepped into a spacious room with half-paneled walls and flocked wallpaper. A man was sitting with his back turned, studying the blueprints and pages of notes strewn over the table.

Without looking up, he murmured, "One moment, Etches. Doctor O'Loughlin won't mind if I'm a bit late for dinner."

Emily cleared her throat. "Are you Mr. Andrews? I'm Emily Cowen. There's something very important I have to ask you about the *Titanic*."

Mr. Andrews straightened and turned around. His face was intelligent and kindly. "Indeed!"

74

He seemed surprised, but not annoyed. "It must be a serious question on your young mind."

"It's a matter of life and death," said Emily bluntly. "Did you know the *Titanic* is sailing straight toward some icebergs? The captain has gotten messages about them. What would happen if the ship hit one?"

"Hm." A faint smile crossed Andrews's face. "To tell you the truth, I've been thinking more about coathooks than icebergs. Of course, if Captain Smith knows that icebergs are about, he'll have the lookouts keep a sharp watch for them. But to set your mind at rest, let me show you the safety features of the *Titanic*." He beckoned Emily over to the table.

The bottom of the *Titanic*, Mr. Andrews explained, was divided into sixteen watertight compartments. He pointed to a plan of the ship as he talked. If an iceberg punctured the hull, the captain would press an electric button. (Andrews said that impressively, as if electric buttons were the latest invention.) Then all the watertight doors between the compartments would automatically close.

Emily could hardly stand still or keep quiet, listening to all this stuff that wasn't going to help in the end. "But what if the iceberg really smashed the ship up?"

"An accident so serious that *two* of the compartments were flooded? That would be unlikely," answered Andrews patiently. "But the ship would still float. The *Titanic* is equipped with an excellent pumping system."

There was something about this man, thought Emily, that reminded her of Matt — maybe his noble, fair-minded look. "But what if the ship *was* sinking," she pressed, "and everyone had to get into the lifeboats?"

"Oh, it wouldn't come to that," Andrews assured her. "The captain would signal another ship with the wireless, and they'd steam over and pick us up."

Emily let out her breath in a groan. How could she force this kindly, reasonable man to imagine the terrible accident ahead?

There was a knock on the door, and the steward who had directed Emily to A-36 stepped in. "I'm sorry to be a few minutes late, Mr. Andrews. I was required to — "

"Never mind, Etches." Andrews smiled at the steward. "I was busy, myself." He nodded politely to Emily. "I hope I've set your mind at rest, Miss Cowen."

"*At rest?*" repeated Emily. She felt herself shaking, like a rocket about to take off. In the back of her mind, a nervous voice like Matt's said, Don't blow it, Emily.

But Emily had had it with being so polite and careful. "How can you think you know so much, when you don't even know that this ship really could sink? And a lot of people would drown! And it would be your fault!"

As Emily shouted, the steward grasped her arms from behind and steered her out the door. She caught one last glimpse of Andrews, looking as if he didn't have a clue why this crazy girl was yelling at him.

"I wonder very much, miss, whether you belong in first class," the steward hissed in her ear. "However, I shall not report the incident, on condition that you depart from this section *immediately*." He closed the stateroom door in her face.

Emily stood in the foyer, crumpling handfuls of the skirt of her green velvet dress. She was beginning to see how the accident must have happened. It had happened because everyone who could have prevented it, including the captain of the *Titanic*, the shipbuilder, and passengers rich enough to buy the *Titanic*, was sure it was impossible.

For the first time, Emily wished she hadn't insisted on going off by herself. She wished she knew where to find Matt, or even Jonathan. She wished she knew how they were doing, so she wouldn't think it all depended on her.

A sound from inside Mr. Andrews's stateroom made Emily jump. She'd better move, before she got thrown out of first class. Emily glanced back at the corridor she'd come from, then trotted across the foyer in the opposite direction.

Stepping through an open door, Emily found herself in a room as large as the first-class lounge, only darker. It was like a den, with mahogany paneling and stained glass windows. The air was hazy, and Emily smelled cigars.

Three men lounged in one of the groupings of leather sofas and armchairs. Smoking and chatting, they didn't seem to notice Emily sneaking into a chair in a dark corner.

I should calm down and try again, thought Emily. Maybe one of these men would pay attention to her. She'd listen to them until she was sure of which one.

"Who'd care to place a bet on when we'll reach New York?" drawled a lazy voice. "I have it on good authority that they expect to break the record for the Queenstown–New York run."

Break the record, with icebergs ahead! Hidden in her wingback chair, Emily gave a silent snort.

"Good authority?" jibed another man. "Who might that be — the Chief Steward?"

There were chuckles. A third voice said, "The Chief Steward is the very *best* authority. He knows more about the ship than old E. J. Smith does."

"Never mind authority," said the second man. "I trust only in my lucky numbers."

Before Emily could introduce herself, and try to persuade these men to do something about the ship, one of the men put down his glass with a clink and stood up. "Shall we meet here after dinner for a game of bridge, gentlemen?" The others rose, too, and they all strolled out of the smoking room.

Emily was disappointed, but she supposed she could wait here until they came back from dinner. Although Emily hated waiting around. Were first-class dinners the kind that took hours? Probably.

Emily wandered around the empty smoking room, staring at the stained glass windows, ducking behind a sofa when a waiter appeared to empty ashtrays.

Emily tried not to think of the *Titanic* steaming full speed ahead through the night. She herself had run out of steam. Yawning in the stuffy air, she slumped into one of the soft, roomy leather armchairs.

7.
A Well-Run Ship

Matt watched Emily disappear through the revolving door. He shrugged, then grinned. His sister was determined, that was for sure. She'd sold more Girl Scout cookies than anyone else in her grade — she just might persuade some millionaires to get very worried about their safety on the *Titanic*.

Swinging his arms, Matt strode on past the skylight dome over the first-class entrance. Already he felt like the captain of a winning team. How could he and Jonathan and Emily help saving the *Titanic*, now that they were actually on board? One of them was bound to succeed. Hang on, Grandpa! thought Matt. We'll be back soon, with the good news.

Pausing near the forward-most smokestack, Matt put his head back to squint at the black-tipped tower. He hadn't imagined that the *Titanic*, every part of it, would seem so big.

Matt knew that the *Titanic* was almost nine

hundred feet long. A sixth of a mile. But it was one thing to know those numbers. It was another thing to stand on the top deck of this floating city. The biggest ship Matt had ever been on was the Staten Island ferry — a rowboat, compared with this monster ship.

To Matt's right was a row of lifeboats. There were only twenty lifeboats on the ship, not nearly enough for the *Titanic*'s two thousand-plus passengers and crew. *If only the* Titanic *had carried enough lifeboats, every single person on board could have been saved.*

Well, that "if only" was one Matt couldn't do anything about. But the lifeboats wouldn't matter, as long as Matt and Emily and Jonathan succeeded.

Letting himself through a wire gate, Matt walked on to the end of the deck. To his left was a large roofed space, protected from the weather by a front wall of glass panels, but open on both sides. Here was the bridge, the control room of the ship.

This was where Matt would find the officers, maybe Captain Smith if he was lucky. This was where Matt would work on the most important "if only": *If only the officers of the* Titanic *had paid more attention to the warnings about icebergs.*

Some moments in history, Matt figured, could easily have gone one way or the other. In the history books, the *Titanic* had sunk. But if just one of the officers on the ship had done things a little differently, the *Titanic* would have been saved. It couldn't be that hard to make a *little* difference.

And there was a man in an officer's uniform, gazing out over the bow of the ship. As Matt opened his mouth to speak, the officer turned. He had a boyish face with a turned-up nose and an alert expression.

"What's this?" the man demanded. "Are you lost, lad? The bridge is off limits to passengers."

"I know, sir," said Matt, "but I was hoping I could talk to one of the officers."

"Officers on duty don't have time for boys," said the man sternly. But there was a little smile at the corners of his mouth, and he motioned Matt to come with him.

They stepped inside a glass-fronted room, where an older officer stood beside the man handling the ship's wheel. The young officer pushed Matt forward. "Requesting permission to show a seastruck young lad around the bridge, sir."

The senior officer nodded with a straight face. "Very well, Mr. Lowe. This is an uneventful watch." He went on to Matt, "You want to be a sailor when you grow up, do you?"

"Yes, sir," said Matt, crossing his fingers behind his back. Actually, he wanted to be a TV news reporter. But this was the wrong time to tell the truth.

"Take my advice, then," said Lowe, "and finish your schooling first. I ran away to sea against my dad's wishes, and look where I am today." He laughed.

The senior officer smiled. "Yes, look where you are: Fifth Officer on the *Titanic*. Not bad for a runaway lad."

"Well, then," said Fifth Officer Lowe to Matt. "As you must know, we are in the wheelhouse." He waved a hand at the ship's wheel. "That man, the quartermaster, steers the ship. I give him his orders, Chief Officer Wilde" — he nodded toward the senior officer — "gives me my orders, and the captain commands all of us, of course."

Matt saw a chance to bring up his subject. "But what if there were an emergency, like right now, and you didn't have time to wait for the captain's orders?"

"Of course, the captain can't be on the bridge at all times," agreed Lowe. "In that case, the officers on duty would have to act on their own."

"So," Matt went on, trying to sound casual, "what would happen right now, if the lookout saw an iceberg ahead?"

"Hm, an iceberg," said Lowe, as if that were an interesting but not really worrisome possibility. "Of course we would have seen it, too. The lookout in the crow's nest is an extra precaution, but we all keep a lookout ourselves. That's what I was just doing on the bridge. In any case, first, the lookout would ring the warning bell three times. Then he'd telephone us from the crow's nest and tell the officer on duty what he'd seen."

"And then?" asked Matt eagerly. This was his chance. This was where they'd made one of the fatal mistakes, trying to steer around the iceberg.

"Then, if it were up to me, I'd order the quartermaster" — Lowe motioned to the man at the wheel — "to steer around the berg."

"But what if you didn't catch sight of the iceberg until the ship was just about to hit it?" Matt tried to keep a respectful tone. "Shouldn't you let her ram it head on?"

Lowe gave Matt a startled smile. "Mr. Wilde, sir," he said to the Chief Officer, "this lad's been reading Knight's *Modern Seamanship*!"

Wilde nodded, looking amused. "Quite right, my boy," he told Matt. "If there's no chance of avoiding a collision, best to let her take it on the bow. The ship's strongest that way. In such a case, I'd signal the engine room to make full speed astern, to slow her down as much as possible."

Matt smiled with relief. So Chief Officer Wilde and Fifth Officer Lowe did understand what to do to save the *Titanic*. Maybe Matt had made the all-important little difference. It might be enough, just to talk about icebergs and remind the officers what ought to be done when the ship met the iceberg tonight.

Lowe beckoned Matt back out to the bridge. "Come along. I'll show you the instruments we were talking about."

The open-sided bridge, Matt noticed now, was lined with equipment, shining with new brass. Lowe explained to him the use of the three telegraphs to the engine room far below, the ship's compass on the binnacle in front of the wheelhouse, the four telephones. He also pointed out the lever that controlled the watertight doors to shut off the compartments below.

Lowe led Matt back into the wheelhouse. "Look on for a bit. In a while, I can show you our course."

As Lowe spoke with Chief Officer Wilde, Matt peered at a notice posted on the wall. It was from the White Star Line, the company that owned the *Titanic* — a list of regulations. They were very long and wordy, but Matt read a few phrases underlined in red.

Safety outweighing every other consideration, it said. There was also a warning against *over-confidence, a most fruitful source of accident*, and again an urging for *safety in navigation*. Matt wondered whether the officers had bothered to read this notice.

The sun, near the western horizon now, glared in the big windows of the wheelhouse. There was something majestic about this mighty ship, steaming toward the setting sun. Matt felt quietly proud of his role in saving it.

Finally Fifth Officer Lowe got free of his duties again and took Matt into the chart room. He leaned over the table, where a kind of ocean map was spread out. "You see, here we are in the North Atlantic. Almost on a latitude with New York. We're southeast of Newfoundland now. Sparks is picking up the Cape Race station on the wireless."

Matt thought it wouldn't hurt to mention the danger ahead again. "And where are the icebergs?"

Reaching across the table, Lowe flicked a slip of paper tucked into the edge of a frame. It had one word on it, *Ice*, and some scribbled figures. "That's Fourth Officer Boxhall's note. Look here, he's marked the position on the chart. The ice is fairly in our path. We'll reach the area about nine-thirty."

"So you'll slow the ship down and watch very carefully tonight?" urged Matt.

Lowe gave Matt an odd look. "The captain sets the speed of the ship, as he sees fit. In any case, I won't be on watch, by that hour." He looked cheerful. "I'll be dead asleep in my bunk by then."

Lowe wasn't on duty tonight! Matt could have kicked himself. How could he have overlooked an important thing like that? Of course, the officers took turns being in charge of the bridge. Matt had wasted a lot of time, giving suggestions and reminders to the wrong officers. Now that he thought of it, he even knew from books he'd read who would be in charge at 11:40 tonight: First Officer Murdoch.

Matt thanked the Fifth Officer for the tour of the bridge and returned through the wheelhouse to the open deck. He'd come back to the bridge to talk to Murdoch later. For now, he'd work on another "if only": *If only the lookouts had had binoculars.*

Matt climbed two flights down a narrow stairway. Then around to the front of B deck and down steps to the well deck, then forward and up more steps to the forecastle deck. Here was the forward mast. And way up there — Matt tilted his head back — was the crow's nest.

As Matt paused, a man in a dark knitted cap and a navy pea jacket stepped down from an iron ladder inside the mast. He wasn't much taller than Matt, and he looked to be in his twenties. " 'Ere now, what're you up to?" he exclaimed at the sight of Matt.

"I'm trying to find Mr. Fleet, the lookout," said Matt. He wasn't going to make the mistake of talking to the wrong lookout.

With a suspicious frown, the man folded his arms across his wool jacket. "I'm Fred Fleet," he declared in his broad Cockney accent. "On my way to the mess for a 'ot meal."

"Great!" exclaimed Matt. "I've got something for you." He lifted the binoculars from around his neck. "I thought you might be able to use these tonight."

Fleet stared. " 'Ow'd you know they didn't give the lookouts no glasses? Word gets around, don't it? I *told* Mr. Lightoller, I says to him, 'We needs the glasses in the crow's nest more than you does on the bridge.' But 'e wouldn't listen to me, 'e wouldn't."

Taking the binoculars from Matt, the lookout held them up to his eyes and aimed them at the top of the mast. He gave a murmur of appreciation.

Matt also gazed up at the mast, a tall silhouette against the darkening sky. He hugged himself — the temperature had dropped from sharp to bitter cold. "Well, good luck tonight." He started to turn back toward the steps to the well deck.

"Oh, no — I couldn't take them fancy glasses." Fleet held them out. "Mr. Lightoller wouldn't like it if 'e got wind I had glasses up there, after all. 'E'd think I'd nicked 'em from a passenger. Thanking you just the same."

Matt couldn't believe this. "Just take them,

okay? Couldn't you hide them somewhere until you go back to the crow's nest?"

"Maybe I could do that." Fleet looked worried, but he pulled his hand back slowly and slid the binoculars into his coat pocket. "But I wouldn't want to get into trouble with the Second Officer. Mr. Lightoller, he doesn't take any nonsense."

Fleet disappeared into the forecastle, and Matt climbed down to the well deck. "Nonsense" for the lookouts to have binoculars — what kind of a stupid idea was that? Never mind. Matt had taken care of one "if only," at least.

8.
"We Never Had It So Good"

Matt paused on the well deck, wondering what to do next. He was cold and hungry. And he wasn't nearly as confident as when he'd first landed on the *Titanic*. The hours were ticking by — it was nighttime, now. But it would be a while before he could meet First Officer Murdoch on the bridge.

A group of men stood near the railing, smoking. The deck lights shone on their mustached faces and their worn clothes. This deck was for the third-class passengers, Matt remembered.

One of the men glanced Matt's way, and he stepped forward. "Excuse me, do you know if they're still serving dinner?"

The other men turned and looked, making remarks in another language. The first man shrugged and smiled at Matt, as if to say he wished he could help.

"Thanks anyway." With a wave Matt walked around a hatch and through a door to a stairway.

He'd find the third-class dining room for himself. In third class, he hoped, nobody would notice if he joined the crowd and had something to eat.

But it wasn't so easy to find the third-class dining room, which Matt had never noticed on the ship's plan in his book. He wandered around corridors and up and down stairs, catching maddening whiffs of stew. How did the real third-class passengers find their way around? Especially if they didn't speak English?

Finally Matt got directions from a passing stewardess. As he came down a last flight of stairs onto F deck, he could hear the rattling and clinking of tableware and crockery. Sure enough, he was right at the entrance to the dining rooms. Oh, no! The rooms were empty, except for waiters clearing the tables.

By desperate pleading, Matt got the waiters to let him take a couple of rolls still left in the baskets. "But don't think you can eat any time you like," warned a dour-looking man. "This is steerage, not first class."

"Never mind him, lad," said a waiter with receding hair and a more friendly expression. He offered Matt butter for his rolls, and poured him a cup of strong tea with milk. "Third class on the *Titanic* is as good as first class on other steamers, eh?"

That must be true, thought Matt. He'd expected third-class meals to be something like the lunches in the cafeteria at his school. But in this white-paneled dining room they had linen tablecloths and napkins, like a nice restaurant. And really good food, if the rolls were a fair sample.

Munching the last roll as he climbed back up the stairs to E deck, Matt remembered another "if only": *If only the third-class passengers had gotten to the boat deck while the lifeboats were loading.* It was easy for Matt to see one reason why they hadn't: They didn't know the way, and the ship was such a huge, confusing place.

If Matt and his team couldn't save the *Titanic*, the passengers in third class had the most to lose. Several of the lifeboats had been lowered only partly full. If more people were ready to get in the boats, it made sense that more people would be saved.

Matt found himself in the broad, long corridor on E deck, in a two-way stream of passengers and crew members. He thought he remembered that the third class had a common room, like a lounge. That was probably the best place to talk to a lot of people, to get them thinking about emergencies and how they'd find the lifeboat deck.

Matt had to flag down another steward to find out where the common room was — near the stern. Heading for the back of the ship, he wove his way through waiters and stewards, engineers and stokers, as well as all the third-class passengers.

A few of the people traveling third class looked pretty much like the first-class passengers above, minus the furs and jewels. But some looked very different. That group with broad faces and high cheekbones, for instance, maybe Russian; the women wore head scarves and peasant skirts. Or that family of Middle Easterners in robes, the wife with a shawl over her head and a baby wrapped in a corner of the shawl. A babble of languages washed around Matt's ears.

The long corridor ended in a low-ceilinged open space at the foot of a steep stairway. Matt followed the traffic up two flights of stairs, toward the sound of a lively piano and fiddle. In one of the large rooms at the top of the stairway, there seemed to be a party going on. The room was crowded, mostly with young adults, singing along with the musicians or talking in clusters.

Matt looked around for a likely person to strike up a conversation with. A young man next to him, tall, blond, and ruddy-faced, smiled and nodded.

"How're you doing?" said Matt. "Matt Cowen." He stuck out his hand.

The young blond man shook his hand. "August Wennerstrom. No English."

That was the end of that conversation, although Wennerstrom kept smiling and motioned Matt in front of him so he could see better. There was a circle of dancers in the middle of the room, doing some kind of folk dance.

"This is the life, eh, Paddy?" remarked a young man beside Matt to his companion. They both wore tweed suits with vests, and tweed caps. "When you think how me uncle came over on the boat to America, and them all crammed together like cattle."

"They do say they sometimes actually used the steerage space for cattle," said Paddy. "I couldn't believe me eyes on this ship, when I saw it was just the four of us to a room, and a washbasin with runnin' water!"

"We never had it so good, at home," agreed the first man.

English speakers! Matt eagerly introduced himself and shook hands. The first man was Daniel. He and Paddy were both from County Mayo, Ireland.

Paddy promptly took Matt to the bar next door, in the third-class smoking room, and treated him to lemonade. By the time they returned to the party, a bagpipe player had taken over the entertainment. Daniel was talking with some other young Irish men and women. They welcomed Matt, slapping him on the back. Over the skirling of the pipes they shouted jokes and

94

stories and described how they'd make their fortunes in America.

Matt listened, smiling weakly and feeling worse and worse. He couldn't help wondering if any of them would survive, and which ones. Finally he gave up waiting for anything like the topic of lifeboats to come up.

"Did you know the ship's gotten a lot of warnings about icebergs?" Matt asked in a loud voice. When he saw he had their surprised attention, he went on. "That's what I heard. I was wondering, how could we get up to the lifeboats, if the *Titanic* hit an iceberg?"

Daniel and Paddy stared at him, then glanced at each other and burst out laughing. "Do you think you're in a little rowboat, lad?" Daniel gave Matt's shoulder a friendly nudge.

"This ship is as likely to sink as Croagh Patrick, the holy mountain," declared Paddy. "She's brand-new, y'know, and built at the finest shipyard in Belfast."

"Besides," a pink-cheeked woman chimed in, "do you think they keep no watch for icebergs and such?"

Matt felt his face grow warm. Daniel and Paddy went back to chatting with the others. Maybe, thought Matt, he should try to find some third-class passengers who weren't having such a good time.

Then Matt noticed a young woman and a little redheaded boy in front of him in the crowd. They clapped and laughed and did a few steps in place to the jig a fiddle was playing. "Don't make me leave the fun, Aunt Rose," begged the boy.

"Just this one jig, and then straight to bed, Frankie," the woman warned.

Another young woman, laughing, tapped Frankie's aunt. "Rose Kenny, did y'know there's a young man from Sweden who has his eye on you?"

Frankie Kenny. Matt felt suddenly breathless. And that curly red hair, just like Emily's. In fact, Frankie could pass for Matt and Emily's little brother.

Instead, he was — he had to be — their great-grandfather.

Matt's chest ached. He leaned forward, longing to tell Frankie who he was, tell him that he and Emily and Jonathan were here on a secret mission, like guardian angels.

But then Jonathan's narrow face, his mouth dropped open in horror, flashed in Matt's mind. *Don't go near your great-grandfather! . . . You might never be born.*

Matt gulped. He wanted to change the past, but not that way. He edged sideways through the crowd, away from Rose and Frankie Kenny, keeping his eyes on the young boy as though he were a dangerous animal. He was relieved when

Frankie and his aunt left the common room a few minutes later.

For the next hour or so, Matt made his way from one group to another, trying to strike up conversations about safety on the *Titanic*. It was hopeless.

Many of the people in the common room, like August Wennerstrom, didn't even speak English. The others weren't any more interested than Daniel or Paddy in how to find the lifeboats. Only a few people would let Matt explain his worry, and they seemed to think that he was overwrought. "Go to bed, lad," was advice he got more than once.

Finally the bar closed. "It's not yet ten o'clock," protested Paddy. But the stewards began to turn out lights and shoo the merry-makers out of the common room. I've only got about two more hours, thought Matt.

As he climbed back down the stairs to E deck, it seemed to Matt that the ceiling was very low. His throat felt tight, as if he were watching the door of a trap close. He was glad it was time for him to go above to the bridge. William Murdoch, the First Officer of the *Titanic*, would be coming on duty there now.

Pretending to be heading for his bunk with the single men, Matt followed the long corridor on E deck back toward the bow of the ship. Then he sneaked away up the stairs, into the icy air of the well deck, and retraced his steps back up to the bridge.

By the dim lights on the bridge, Matt saw two officers outside the wheelhouse. They were gazing over the bow through the glass screen. One of them held a pair of binoculars. "Very clear tonight, Mr. Lightoller," said the other man.

"Extremely clear, Mr. Murdoch," said Second Officer Lightoller. His voice was deep and confident. "You can see the stars setting right at the horizon." The two men were silent for a moment. Just as Matt was wondering whether to break in, Lightoller went on, "The temperature has dropped twelve degrees since I came on watch. I've told the lookouts to keep a sharp watch for small ice and growlers. We should be getting up around the ice any time now."

"Yes," said Murdoch. "Earlier, I had the lamp trimmer fasten the forward forecastle hatch, so the light wouldn't interfere with the view from the crow's nest. The sea is so calm, I don't suppose we'd see breakers about the foot of a berg."

Matt couldn't hold himself back anymore. "Excuse me, sir." He stepped out of the shadows. "That's just how an accident could happen. You wouldn't see the iceberg until it was too late. So don't you think you should slow the ship down?"

Both officers stared at Matt, Lightoller with a frown. "I apologize," he told the First Officer.

"I don't know how they let this boy on the bridge."

Murdoch held up his hand, looking amused. "Never mind, Mr. Lightoller. My boy," he went on to Matt, "I didn't say we wouldn't be able to see the *iceberg* — only that there wouldn't be any breakers at its foot. There would be a certain amount of reflected light from the berg itself."

"Yes," said Lightoller, although he looked as if he didn't approve of discussing the matter with a passenger. "Even if it were a newly split-off iceberg, presenting its dark-blue side to us, we would see a white outline around it."

First Officer Murdoch nodded. "Unless, as the captain was saying, it becomes at all hazy. Then we should have to go very slowly." He finished pointedly, "*Good night,* young man. Good night, Mr. Lightoller."

"Good night, Mr. Murdoch." Second Officer Lightoller handed him the binoculars. "I'll finish my rounds, and then I'm off to sweet dreams." Turning to Matt, he added, "We run a tight ship. If this were my watch, I'd have a seaman march you to your cabin so fast, your head would spin."

Matt took the hint and left. But he didn't know whether he'd accomplished anything or not. Mr. Murdoch — all the officers, in fact — seemed well informed about the icebergs ahead. Maybe Matt had already made the all-important little difference to save the *Titanic*, just by talk-ing to First Officer Lowe this afternoon. Any-way, the binoculars he'd given to the lookout should be enough to prevent the accident.

Hugging himself against the bitter cold, Matt wandered aft. He passed the officers' quarters, the forward row of lifeboats, the first-class en-trance over the Grand Stairway. He wondered how Emily was doing in first-class territory. What if she'd gotten locked in someone's cabin, and couldn't get out by midnight?

And what about Jonathan, down below? What if they'd caught him trying to stop an engine, and thrown him in the brig? Matt hadn't thought this through very carefully.

On an impulse Matt turned back, pushed through the revolving door of the first-class en-trance, and made his way below. He didn't have a clue where Emily would be, by now, but Jon-athan might not be hard to check up on. If Matt just caught a glimpse of his friend, to know he was okay, he could relax until they met at mid-night.

Reaching F deck, Matt found a door marked CREW ONLY that opened onto an iron stairway. He started down the steps into the smoky air and the racket of the *Titanic*'s engines. But then he paused.

Matt was tired, his head ached, and he didn't seem to be thinking clearly. What if Jonathan was all set to stop the *Titanic* — and then Matt's appearance messed up his plan? What if they were *both* caught and thrown in the brig?

Matt peered down into the thick air of the boiler rooms. It wouldn't be as easy as he'd thought, to spot Jonathan. He couldn't see very far.

Somehow this thought caused an image to float into Matt's mind. A pair of binoculars.

Matt felt as cold as if he'd fallen into the icy Atlantic. He stared at his watch. It was eleven-thirty.

Scrambling back up the iron steps, Matt dashed down the corridor and up six flights of stairs to the bridge.

9.
Collision

Matt stopped just outside the bridge shelter area. There was First Officer Murdoch, talking with a junior officer and a seaman.

And there were the binoculars — *Matt's binoculars* — hanging beside the telegraph equipment. Second Officer Lightoller must have taken them away from Lookout Fleet.

Matt leapt through the open doorway. "Mr. Murdoch! Stop the ship! There's going to be an accident!"

With hardly a raised eyebrow, the First Officer barked at the seaman. "Remove that boy from — "

Murdoch was interrupted by the *ding-ding-ding* of a brass bell far overhead. The telephone on the wall rang, and the junior officer picked it up. "What did you see?" he asked calmly. A pause, then, "Thank you." To Murdoch he said, "Iceberg right ahead, sir."

"Hard a-starboard!" called Murdoch to the quartermaster steering the ship.

"No, don't turn!" exclaimed Matt. He lunged through the door toward the wheel. But the quartermaster was already swinging the wheel around as far as it would go. He put a quick elbow in Matt's stomach without moving from his post.

Outside the wheel room, Murdoch spoke in a choked voice. "There's the berg. Full speed astern."

"Full speed astern," repeated the junior officer. He yanked down the lever to send the signal to the engine room. The telegraph bells clanged.

Then the seconds crawled by. Clutching his sore stomach, Matt staggered out of the wheel house. He stared at the massive shadow looming up from the sea. The bow of the ship swung slowly to the left.

There was a grinding jar.

In the first-class smoking room on A deck, Emily woke up. She felt as if she'd only slept for a minute. But men were talking and laughing in the room again. Ice clinked in glasses. Three or four groups were playing cards — Emily could hear the decks being shuffled. In a nearby part of the ship, the band played a ragtime tune.

The voice of Mr. Lucky Numbers spoke from

the table nearest Emily. "How about it, gentlemen? When are we going to reach New York?"

Then she felt a bump. Nothing much — as if something had only tapped the outside of the ship.

"Hullo," said one of the men near Emily. None of them got up.

But Emily leapt to her feet. Following a steward and a young man, she ran out of the smoking room. They charged past an indoor patio of palm trees and ivy and burst out onto the deck.

The iceberg was *right there*. A dark blue mountain, higher than the top deck, scraping along the side of the ship. Suddenly the *Titanic* was not the biggest thing on the ocean. The deck lights glinted off glassy crags as the iceberg seemed to slide backward. Huge lumps of ice cracked off and splashed into the water far below.

"We hit an iceberg!" shouted someone. "There it is!"

Emily felt as though a chunk of the ice had landed in her stomach. The iceberg was past the stern of the *Titanic* now. Its dark bulk blotted out the stars for a moment. Then it was gone.

Down in boiler room number six, an alarm bell shrilled. The red light above the door began flashing. "It's full speed astern!" shouted Engineer Hesketh.

Jonathan's heart pounded so hard, he felt sick.

Calm down, he tried to tell himself. Maybe the alarm meant the *Titanic* was saved. Maybe Matt had gotten the officers to watch out for the ice, after all. Maybe Emily had gotten some nervous millionaires so scared of icebergs that they'd made the captain stop the ship.

"Shut down the dampers!" yelled Fred to the stokers. They jumped to the furnaces.

But the stokers had only been working for a moment when there was a massive *thud*. Then a shuddering, grinding noise.

"Blimey!" exclaimed Fred.

A waterfall of ocean gushed into the boiler room. Fred jumped onto an escape ladder. Hesketh dove for the watertight door, which was sliding down like a slow meat slicer. Jonathan plunged after the engineer, rolling under the door just before it slammed shut.

Water was rushing into this boiler room, too. More like an open fire hydrant than a waterfall, but the floor was awash already. Jonathan, soaking wet, pushed himself to his feet.

I'm going to drown down here, thought Jonathan in a daze. I *told* Matt and Emily it was a big enough deal, just to travel in time. I *told* them it was too much, trying to save —

"Man the pumps," barked Hesketh. Men dragged in heavy hoses. "We've struck an iceberg!" came a shout from above.

Fred dropped into boiler room number five from a ladder. Noticing Jonathan, he jerked his head toward the escape ladder. "Up top, lad. Go on."

With trembling arms, Jonathan began hauling himself up the wall. Now that he had a chance to escape, it seemed cowardly to leave. But he couldn't help here, and Matt and Emily couldn't use the TASC without him. In the corridor on F deck, Jonathan patted the TASC control, miraculously still in his pocket.

Out of the steam and smoke of the boiler rooms, Jonathan's head seemed to clear. It wasn't quite time to meet Matt and Emily yet. And there was one more thing he could do for his mission. The *Titanic* might be doomed, but there was still a chance to save the *people* on the *Titanic*.

If only another ship could be signaled in time. Now, the one hope left was the wireless.

10.
Women and Children First

For the first few moments after the collision, Matt stood paralyzed outside the wheelhouse. We failed, he thought.

The next thought smacked his mind as if someone had hit him on the side of the head: *We could all go down with the ship*.

Before Matt could move, Captain Smith was on the bridge. Matt recognized the white-bearded captain from his picture in the book. But he would have known, anyway, that this was the man in charge.

As the captain asked questions and gave orders in a quietly forceful tone, Matt began to feel more hopeful. This was all too calm to be the scene of an emergency. And if the *Titanic* had really been wrecked, it would have been a much bigger crash — wouldn't it? He breathed out a long sigh and picked his binoculars from the hook.

"The watertight doors are closed?" asked the

captain of Murdoch. He turned to a steward. "Request Mr. Andrews to come to the bridge as soon as he can."

Mr. Andrews, thought Matt. The manager of the shipbuilding company who built the *Titanic*. He'd be able to tell whether the ship was badly damaged.

Then a man with a handlebar mustache, coat thrown over his pajamas and slippers flapping, hurried up to Captain Smith. Matt caught the name "Ismay." That must be J. Bruce Ismay, the chairman of the White Star Line.

Ismay seemed to have a hard time believing that the ship had really collided with an iceberg. He sputtered out question after question. But the captain turned away as soon as Andrews appeared.

Matt followed Captain Smith and Andrews, still in his evening clothes, off the bridge. "Best take the crew's stairway," the captain told Andrews, "so as not to alarm the passengers."

Seven decks down from the bridge, they met clerks dragging sodden bags out of the mail room. Peering into the squash court next door, Matt saw water lapping the foul line. A lot of water was leaking in, for a ship that wasn't wrecked.

Farther aft, Andrews descended a ladder and spoke with the engineers and stokers below. He returned with a grim face. "Number six boiler room is completely flooded. They're pumping number five, but it looks bad."

Captain Smith nodded. The calm, in-command expression on his white-bearded face did not change, but he turned without a word.

Matt trailed behind the captain and Andrews as they headed back up. He had a sense of the *Titanic* as a live thing, an enormous beast. He and the captain and Andrews were like microbes scurrying through her.

At the bottom of the first-class stairs on E deck, Andrews said, "The first five compartments are flooded."

"But the watertight doors were shut," said Captain Smith. He still sounded calm — or maybe stunned.

"The berg must have ripped a three-hundred-foot gash," said Andrews. "Through the number one hold, the number two hold, the mail room, and the first two boiler rooms." He shook his head.

In the corridors on C deck, first-class passengers in nightgowns and pajamas were sticking their heads out of their cabins. Captain Smith nodded and smiled at them. To Andrews, he said, "What does this mean?"

"The watertight doors would keep her afloat if only two compartments were flooded — three, maybe four." Andrews kept his face smooth and his voice low. "But with five gone, the water will pull the bow down so far that the rest of the compartments will flood, one after the other."

"The *Titanic* is unsinkable," said the captain in a dazed voice.

"The *Titanic* is sinking," answered the builder. "I give her an hour and a half. Perhaps two hours."

Matt looked at the captain for his reaction, but Captain Smith marched steadily on up the next flight of stairs. "I must tell the wireless operators to call for assistance. Have the lifeboats uncovered. Summon all passengers and crew on deck."

"We must be careful not to alarm them," said Andrews.

"No, there must be no panic," agreed the captain. "Women and children first." He strode briskly through the A deck foyer, already crowded with first-class passengers. They all gazed at the captain, and he nodded greetings right and left on his way to the Grand Staircase. Andrews crossed the foyer in the direction of the lounge, stopping here and there to say a word to the passengers.

No panic, Matt told himself as he followed the captain up the last flight of stairs. His heart was thudding. Emily! Jonathan! They had to get off this sinking ship. He glanced at the ornamented clock on the landing of the Grand Staircase. It was 12:10.

Out on the boat deck, a thunderous blast, like the roar of a wounded monster, filled the air. Matt gazed up. Huge clouds billowed out of the funnels, blotting the starry sky.

"Don't be afraid," explained a nearby gentleman to his lady companion. "She's only letting off steam."

As Matt hurried past the aft row of lifeboats, an officer appeared with a group of seamen. They fell to work on the boats, pulling off the canvas covers and cranking the boats out over the railing.

Let them be here, prayed Matt as he reached the stern end of the boat deck. But there was no one in the spot where he and Jonathan and Emily had landed, except a few passengers. They looked confused, but not really frightened. Only one elderly woman wore a life belt, which made her look like an upright turtle.

Matt glanced over the back railing, three decks down into third-class territory. There were people milling around down there. He could hear their puzzled voices, but not the words.

Had young Frank Kenny's Aunt Rose pulled him out of his bunk yet? Matt felt an urge to find out. No. He had to wait here. But where *were* Emily and Jonathan?

A skinny figure with a blackened face dashed down the port side of the deck. It halted, panting, before Matt. "The ship is sinking. The ship is sinking. Let's go!"

Matt stared. "Jonathan! What happened?" His friend was shuddering, and his hair and clothes were wet.

Jonathan stared back out of white-circled eyes. "Man, I almost drowned down there. And then I rushed back up to the wireless room. I told them the boiler rooms are flooded, call another ship for help! They just looked at me, like, 'Gee whiz, how'd you get wet, Jonathan? No, we can't call for help unless the captain tells us to'!"

As Jonathan sputtered and choked for a moment, Matt nodded. "That's the way they acted on the bridge. But hey — did you see Emily anywhere?"

"And *then*," Jonathan blurted on, "then Jack and Harold start explaining to me about the watertight compartments. As if *I* didn't almost get sliced in half a few minutes ago by one of those wonderful watertight doors!"

"I said, 'Did you see Emily?'" Matt reached out to shake his friend.

Jonathan paused, looking puzzled as he finally took in Matt's question. "Emily? Isn't she with you?"

"No. I've got to go find her." Matt was suddenly afraid she'd done what he'd thought of doing, going down to steerage to check on Frank Kenny. "Wait here."

Jonathan was still muttering as Matt pushed him down on a bench. "So then we just sat there in the wireless room until Captain Smith finally showed up. By that time it was *half an hour* after the ship hit the iceberg!"

"I know." Matt wrapped a stray deck blanket around his friend.

"Then" — Jonathan's voice was muffled by the folds of the blanket — "then Jack acts like, 'Gee sir, if you say so, sir, there must be an emergency, sir, so now I'll go ahead and call for help. *Dit-da-dit-da.*'"

Leaving him still muttering, Matt hurried forward, toward the entrance to the Grand Stairway.

Now more passengers were appearing on deck. Near the first-class entrance, a group watched the crew prepare the first lifeboat. An aristocratic-looking man remarked to the young woman clinging to his arm, "We are safer here than in that little boat, my dear."

"The ship is sinking!" Matt snapped at their startled faces. He plunged through the revolving door and down the Grand Staircase once again.

All the lights that had been turned down for the night, including the crystal chandelier, were blazing away now. The foyer was thronged with passengers, as if it were a party. A strange costume party, with half the guests in life jackets. Matt pushed his way through the crowd.

113

One woman wore a dressing gown and a man's overcoat; another wore a stylish suit, but her high-button shoes flapped open. Others had put on long dusters and hats with veils, as if they were going for a ride in the country. A stout man had only pajamas on under his life belt.

Somewhere nearby, a band was playing a lighthearted ragtime tune. A woman's voice rose above the general hum. "I must see the purser," she announced. "All my best jewels are in the ship's safe. Where *is* Mr. McElroy?"

Matt hurried down another flight of stairs to B deck and almost bumped into a steward. "Have you seen a girl with curly red hair, ten years old?" he gasped. "My sister."

"All the first-class passengers have been roused," said the steward. His calm tone implied that everything was under control. "I believe I did see a girl answering to that description. Yes, wearing a green velvet dress."

"That's her!" exclaimed Matt. "Where did she go?"

"I'm sure she would be on the boat deck by now." The steward turned from Matt, as if the subject were closed. He held out a hand to a woman struggling to fasten her life belt. "If I may, madam."

Now Matt was sure Emily must have gone down to steerage. He plunged on down the stairway, three more flights to E deck.

Reaching the long central corridor on E deck, Matt was surprised. There was no one around. Wouldn't all the single men in steerage be leaving their flooded third-class bunks in the bow? This corridor was the fastest way to the third-class quarters in the stern. And he'd expected to see some crew members escaping from the flooded boiler rooms.

As Matt paused, a steward came out of a cabin carrying a heavy jacket. "You'd best go above," he told Matt. He pointed down the corridor toward the bow.

At first Matt wondered why the steward was directing him above by way of the bow. Then he realized the man was warning him, pointing at the water on the floor.

Water, reflecting the light bulb on the ceiling. The forward end of the corridor was a pond.

A cold lump of fear formed at the back of Matt's throat. He whirled and ran aft, not stopping until he reached the end of the corridor.

At the foot of the third-class stairway, Matt found the passengers who'd already left the bow. They huddled together, jostling like sheep, all talking at once in a confusion of languages. Babies wailed.

A steward threaded his way through the crowd, trying to get them to put life belts on. "No, there's nothing wrong," he explained. "No danger at all — just a precaution."

Pushing up the steep stairs, Matt turned to survey the crowd below. There was a gleam of red hair under the scarves on two or three girls' heads, but they weren't Emily's. He climbed on up the two flights to the third-class deck space.

Here another steward was standing on a bench, shouting over the babble. "I'm taking a group up to the lifeboats. Women and children only, please step forward. Women and children *only*, sir. This way, miss, with the little boy."

The young woman had a shawl over her head, and Matt couldn't see her face. But he heard her say to the redheaded boy, "Come along, Frankie, there's a brave lad."

The steward gathered his little flock of women and children and disappeared through a door marked SECOND CLASS ONLY. "Let them all up!" shouted Matt. "It's not fair!" Up above, he knew, lifeboats were being lowered half full.

"Come along, then," said a voice at Matt's elbow. It was Daniel, one of the Irishmen who'd befriended him earlier this evening. "If we wait for them to escort us ever so politely to the lifeboats, we'll drown. Follow Paddy, lad, up those steps. I'll be right behind ye."

Why not? Emily must be above, after all. Matt clambered up after Paddy's thick-soled boots, reached the deck above, and grasped the railing of another set of steps.

"First class only!" shouted a voice from above. "You have your own boats down there."

Matt opened his mouth to shout back that this was baloney. All the *Titanic*'s lifeboats were on the boat deck. But the sailor above shoved Paddy backward. The Irishman fell down the stairs, bumping Matt on the way by.

Matt was afraid Paddy was hurt, but he jumped to his feet and leapt back up the steps like a wild man. There was a crack and crunch of breaking wood.

"Good for Paddy, he's torn down the gate." Dan boosted Matt up the steps, and they scrambled through the broken gate onto the deck.

Then the men looked uncertainly around. They peered in the windows of a fancy restaurant, all lit up. They peered out under the roof of the deck. The ocean gleamed far below.

"Come on!" urged Matt. He pushed ahead and led them forward, toward the foyer and the stairs to the boat deck. As they passed the first-class smoking room, he glanced in the windows. A foursome of gentlemen in evening clothes sat around a table with their cards and drinks. Another man, sunk into a leather armchair, seemed absorbed in his book.

Passing the first-class lounge windows, Matt noticed several more people who weren't even trying to get to the lifeboats. There was an elderly couple sitting quietly on a sofa, clasping each other's hands.

Matt trotted on, with Daniel and Paddy clumping behind him, into the first-class foyer, up the Grand Staircase, and out onto the boat deck. Right ahead of him, Second Officer Lightoller was directing the loading of a lifeboat.

"Please step in, Mrs. Cavendish." Lightoller offered his hand to a woman wearing a dressing gown and a man's overcoat. She turned away from the Second Officer, casting her husband a worried look. He bent down, and they kissed. Then Mr. Cavendish pushed his wife toward the boat and vanished into the crowd.

As Mrs. Cavendish stumbled into the lifeboat, Matt noticed a plump woman in a black velvet suit standing nearby. Her eyes sparkled, as if climbing off an ocean liner into a little boat, in the middle of the night, was her idea of fun. She spoke encouragingly to someone on the other side of her.

"Never fret, dearie," said the plump woman. "Stick with Mrs. Brown — you can find your brother later. He'd want you to hop in a boat soon as you could."

Leaning to peer around Mrs. Brown's ample form, Matt caught a glimpse of red hair. "Emily!"

His sister pulled backward from her friend's

arm. "Matt!" She wiggled through the crowd toward him.

"Come back, Emily!" Mrs. Brown started after her, but two seamen grabbed her by the arms and swung her over the side. There was a squawk and a thud. Then the ropes creaked as the crew began lowering the boat.

Grabbing Emily's arm as if she might try to get away, Matt headed for the stern. He scowled down at her. "Are you crazy! If you'd gone off in that lifeboat — "

"*I* was at our meeting place at midnight!" Emily glared back. "I waited for the longest time. Then I thought I'd better go look for you. But I ran into Mrs. Brown instead, and she grabbed me and said we had to get to a lifeboat."

Emily paused for breath. They struggled through the crush of people near the band. The musicians were now playing their cheerful ragtime outside the first-class entrance.

"And I guess I could have gotten away from Mrs. Brown," Emily went on. "But I didn't know where you were." Her voice sank to an un-Emily-like whisper. "I didn't know what was going to happen."

Matt swallowed hard. He was about to apologize to his sister, in a most un-Matt-like way, when she cut him off.

"Where's Jonathan?" asked Emily. "What if he got stuck down in — "

119

"No, he's waiting for us." Matt hoped that was true. Among other things, Jonathan was the one with the TASC control.

There was a *whoosh* on the other side of the ship, from the bridge. A white flare burst overhead. "They're trying to signal," said Matt.

He remembered another "if only": *If only the* Californian, *a small ocean liner just ten miles away, had received the distress call.* If the *Californian* had known the *Titanic* was sinking, she could have steamed over and saved every person on board. But the *Californian*'s one wireless operator was only on duty until 11:30 P.M. — ten minutes before the *Titanic* hit the iceberg.

"We're walking uphill." Emily's voice shook.

Matt's insides shook, too. There was now a definite tilt to the deck of the *Titanic*.

11.
The Promise

As they neared the back end of the boat deck, Matt scanned the crowd. Jonathan wouldn't have given up on them and gone back by himself — would he?

Matt and Emily dodged around a group waiting to get into another lifeboat. A young mother with two little girls was already down in the boat. "Papa," called the younger girl, about four years old. "Aren't you coming with us?"

A man at the railing smiled and waved to them, as calmly as if he were standing on dry land and watching his family leave on a bus. "I'll come on the next boat," he called back. "Be good girls — mind Mama."

The mother, an arm around each of her girls, stared up from the lifeboat. "Are you sure there's another boat, Samuel?"

Matt pulled Emily away. Over her shoulder, Emily shouted shrilly. "Get in the boat with them!" Then she exclaimed, "Aak!" She'd almost bumped into the tall, sooty-faced figure looming ahead.

His blanket clutched around him, Jonathan stared at them accusingly. "What t-took you so long?" In spite of the blanket, his teeth were chattering.

"Never mind." Matt was glad to see the TASC remote control in Jonathan's free hand. "Let's go."

Matt tugged Emily toward a clear space on the deck, but she pulled away and pointed down over the back railing. "Those poor people!" A line of men were crawling like insects up the crane from the third-class well deck. They inched along the boom toward A deck, first-class space.

"I hope they make it." Matt's voice was choked. He meant Daniel and Paddy, too. He hadn't seen them since they reached the boat deck.

"I hope *we* m-make it," said Jonathan. He took the TASC control from his pocket. "Get over here, in front of this bunch of d-deck chairs."

As he spoke, the ship settled another notch. The chairs rattled, and a couple of them clattered away down the deck. Emily and Matt hastily lined up with Jonathan, the three of them nudging together. Beyond the stern of the ship, the sea was flat calm, reflecting the ship's lights like a mirror. No wake from the *Titanic* broke the pondlike surface — or ever would again, thought Matt.

"D-don't move," said Jonathan.

Matt tried not to shiver. It wasn't easy, now that he was standing still. The cold bit through his pants as if they were made of tissues. He thought how much colder the Atlantic Ocean would feel, if they couldn't escape.

A pistol shot cracked from forward and starboard. "Stand back!" shouted a man's voice. "Women and children first!"

That was Fifth Officer Lowe's voice, realized Matt. Only he didn't sound cheerful anymore. Those poor guys from third class must be trying to get into a lifeboat.

"It's not working," said Jonathan. His breath was coming out in moans.

"Try it again!" snapped Emily. At the same time, Matt asked, "Are you sure you're pressing the right button?"

How much of a chance did the three kids from the future have, if the TASC wouldn't carry them back to their own time? The crew would start loading the backup collapsible lifeboats now. They'd surely find a place for Emily, a girl. But maybe not for two older boys.

Jonathan made a nervous sound, halfway between a cough and a laugh. "I guess I *was* pressing CANCEL instead of TRANSPORT. Hold still again."

Matt's back was to the smokestack, but he felt it towering above them not so far away. One of the *Titanic*'s four smokestacks had fallen over as the ship sank, he remembered. Was it this one?

A tingle ran through Matt. At first he thought it was just from being afraid and cold. Then he recognized that molecule-rearranging feeling.

And then the shouts and cries and footsteps and sounds of creaking wood and rope faded away. And Matt was afraid, and blind and deaf and helpless again. He *whooshed* through nothingness like a pile of leaves in front of a leaf blower. Even though he'd been through this before, he would have screamed his lungs out — if he'd known where his lungs were.

Just as Matt was thinking it would be better to stay on the *Titanic* than to end up like this forever, a bright light shone in his eyes. A pink light. He could hear again — a quiet humming and bubbling.

Matt fell to the carpet with a yelp, not even minding when his head bumped Emily's. Jonathan rolled on his back like a dog, while Emily clutched at the carpet as if she might be dragged back to 1912. Matt pressed his face into the carpet fuzz, and then he sneezed. "Turn it off!"

"Off," agreed Jonathan in a groan. Crawling across Matt's bedroom floor, he pulled the plugs of the Time and Space Connector. The pink light shut off. The bubbling and humming trailed away.

Jonathan lay back on the floor, patting his sweater. "Hey, my clothes aren't wet anymore."

Matt sat up, suddenly feeling awful. Yes, the three of *them* had survived. But all those other people hadn't.

"Mrs. Brown!" Emily burst into howling tears. *"What happened to Mrs. Brown?"*

"Stop that!" Matt was afraid he might start howling, too. "I bet Mrs. Brown was okay. She got into a lifeboat. Shh, shh. We can find out who survived. There's a list." He stood up, shakily, and pulled his book on the *Titanic* out of the projector.

"Yeah, what about the wireless guys?" demanded Jonathan. His deck blanket was gone, Matt noticed, and so was the soot from his face. "Let's see that list."

Jonathan and Emily crowded Matt on either side as he opened the book. The list of passengers and crew was in the back, with the survivors' names in italics. Jonathan stuck his forefinger at the bottom of a page. "Bride, Harold! All right!" He flipped a page, then spoke in a sober voice. "But not Jack Phillips."

"Mrs. Brown made it." Emily let out a long sigh.

"I told you," said Matt. "Now that I think of it, she even took charge of her lifeboat. She cheered them up and ordered them around."

Emily grinned. "That sounds like Mrs. Brown."

They fell silent, searching the list for the names they knew. Matt already knew that Fifth Officer Lowe and Second Officer Lightoller had survived, because they'd both commanded lifeboats. He'd also known that Captain Smith went down with his ship. So did the shipbuilder, Mr. Andrews.

"I saw Mr. Andrews when I was running around trying to find you, Matt," said Emily. "He looked awful. I wish I hadn't told him the accident would be his fault."

"Look at this," said Matt, to distract her. "J. Bruce Ismay — you know, he was the chairman of the White Star Line? — got into a boat somehow."

"That's not fair!" exclaimed Emily. Matt agreed. There was nothing fair about who made it and who didn't.

"Fred Barrett!" Jonathan pounced on the head stoker's name in italics. "How did he get out of that boiler room alive?"

There were a few happy surprises like Fred Barrett, but most of the long, long list was not in italics. Out of the 2,201 passengers and crew members on the *Titanic,* only 705 of them had reached dry land alive.

Matt ran his eyes down the list of third-class passengers. This was the worst part: out of 709, only 176 had survived. Only 81 of 179 women and 23 of 76 children, in spite of all that talk about "women and children first."

Kelly, Kerane, Kennedy — A name popped out at Matt from the third-class list. *Kenny, Francis.*

"Grandpa Frank," he said to Emily. "We've got to tell him."

"Tell him what?" asked Jonathan. "That we failed, trying to carry out his mission?" He snorted. "I can't believe I was so worried about changing the past. We knew what went wrong on the *Titanic,* and we all worked for hours. And we didn't make one micrometer of difference."

"Bingo!" Matt grinned at his friend.

"Yeah, that's what we have to tell him." Emily smiled at Jonathan. "Don't you get it?"

Struggling out of his sport coat and sweater, Matt headed for the door. "Come on."

"Before he gives up," added Emily, dropping her coat.

Jonathan *didn't* seem to get it. "What do you mean, 'tell him'?" But he shed his own extra clothes and followed Matt and Emily down the hall and out the front door.

The mild breeze outside seemed to blow away the icy night of the *Titanic*. With Emily close behind, Matt loped up the hill.

Jonathan caught up, panting, at the Pinesbridge Deli. "What're you going to tell him?" he repeated. "You can't tell him you did what he wanted, stop the *Titanic* from sinking. We did everything we could think of — a lot more than he could've done — and we just couldn't save the ship."

"Right," said Matt, and he loped on. He didn't want to stop to explain.

Pushing the rickety TASC cart from Grandpa Frank's to Matt and Emily's had taken more than half an hour. But now the three kids covered the distance in a few minutes. Matt paused in front of Grandpa Frank's porch, then motioned the others to follow him around to the back door. No need to talk to Mrs. Wilson again.

As they tiptoed into the dark back bedroom, Matt remembered the pill Mrs. Wilson had given the old man. "Grandpa?" Maybe he would be too sedated to wake up.

"Mmp?" Grandpa Frank was still lying on top of the bed, propped up on pillows. He fumbled with the lamp to turn it on, then reached for his glasses. Matt noticed a little white pill on the night table, and he smiled to himself. It looked like the old man had decided not to take his medicine.

Grandpa Frank carefully pushed his glasses onto his face. He squinted at each one of them. "I thought you'd left," he said. "My mind's playing tricks on me. And now you're all dressed up."

"We came back," panted Emily. She bounded onto the bed and paused to catch her breath. "Grandpa, don't get mad, all right? We tried to do what you were going to do, before you broke your leg."

"You what?" The old man was suddenly wide awake and glaring at them. "You'd better be joking. I told you boys not to fiddle with — "

"We were really careful with your invention." Matt dropped into the bedside chair and leaned toward his great-grandfather. "But listen. We found out something very important: *Nobody could save the Titanic.*"

Grandpa Frank stared from Emily on one side of the bed to Matt on the other to Jonathan at the footboard. He touched his hearing aid, as if he thought it must not be working right. "You never got to the ship," he snorted. "How could you have operated my Time and Space Connector? I wasn't so certain it would work for me."

"The TASC worked without a hitch," Jonathan assured him. "Well, one little hitch, coming back. Anyway, you were right about the crystal, Mr. Kenny."

The old man snorted again, flapping a hand at them. He closed his eyes, as if he were tired of their joke.

"You don't believe us," said Matt. Why hadn't he thought of bringing back some kind of proof? But maybe you *couldn't* bring things back through time — Jonathan hadn't even brought the water in his clothes from 1912.

Then Matt realized that he *had* brought something back: new memories. He was gazing at his great-grandfather, a bald-headed man, almost ninety. But now he seemed to see the old man's face through an image of the young boy who'd sailed on the R.M.S. *Titanic*.

"Grandpa," said Matt urgently. "I know something about you, something that you never told us. I know you used to have red hair, when you were a kid."

The old man opened his eyes. Thoughtfully he reached out to Emily and picked up a strand of her curly, carroty hair. "I did, that's a fact. Hair like this."

"And I heard you talking with an Irish accent," Matt went on.

Grandpa Frank smiled a little. "Did ye think I'd be talkin' with a Roosian accent, now?" he asked, putting on an Irish brogue. Then he let out a deep, shuddering sigh. *"You really went to the ship?"* His hand trembled as he put it up to cover his eyes. "I never would have wished you to see that terrible night."

"It *was* terrible," said Emily, "but it was worth it. Grandpa, you didn't pay any attention to what Matt said. We proved that no one could save the *Titanic*."

"Not possible, Mr. Kenny," Jonathan put in. "No way."

"We all went to different parts of the ship," explained Matt, "and we tried everything."

There was silence for a moment. Grandpa Frank stared ahead at the blank TV screen, frowning as if he were struggling with a new idea. "You did this for me," the old man said finally. "You saw what was eating at me, and you wanted to help out." A broad grin spread over the folds and wrinkles of his face. "And you got that contraption of mine to work! Gorry! Aren't you the dickens! The dickens, all three of you!"

"Yeah," said Emily, grinning back.

Jonathan smiled modestly. "It was a simple matter of following your directions, Mr. Kenny. You'd written it all down."

"But do you get it?" Emily asked her great-grandfather. "You couldn't have saved the *Titanic*, either. So don't brood about it anymore."

Grandpa Frank picked up her hand and squeezed it. His eyes looked very bright behind his glasses. "You're good kids," he croaked.

Matt saw a tear run down Emily's chin, and he felt a lump in his own throat. Jonathan squirmed, looking horribly embarrassed.

"But you don't have much sense," barked the old man with sudden force. He swept them with a stern gaze. "That was a very dangerous, very foolhardy thing to do. Now, you're not to go back again, any of you. Do you understand? I can't allow it."

"We won't," promised Matt. That was an easy promise. Who'd want to live through the sinking of the *Titanic* again?

For some reason, Jonathan was making weird faces at Matt, rolling his eyes. Then Matt realized the reason, as temptation whispered in his own mind: *There are lots of adventures in the past besides the sinking of the* Titanic.

"We won't," echoed Emily, but Matt noticed she had one hand behind her back. He'd bet her fingers were crossed.

Matt spoke again, pronouncing his words with careful emphasis: "We promise, we'll never even try to go back . . . to the *Titanic*."